T0209084

Other Books by John D. Drake

Act II: Adventures of a Young Widow
Downshifting: How to Work Less and Enjoy Life More
The Perfect Interview: How to Get the Job You Really Want
How to Drop Five Strokes without Having One
Performance Appraisal: One More Time
The Effective Interviewer
*Interviewing for Managers: A Complete
Guide to Employment Interviewing*
The New Cook's Cookbook (with Sebastian Milardo)
*Finding a Job When Jobs Are Hard to
Find* (with Jurg Oppliger)
A CEO's Guide to Interpersonal Relationships

NEW BLUE

A JERRY KRONE NOVEL

JOHN D. DRAKE
KEVIN C. KOZAK

NEW BLUE
A JERRY KRONE NOVEL

iUniverse books may be ordered through booksellers or by contacting:

iUniverse
1663 Liberty Drive
Bloomington, IN 47403
www.iuniverse.com
844-349-9409

Because of the dynamic nature of the Internet, any web addresses or links contained in this book may have changed since publication and may no longer be valid. The views expressed in this work are solely those of the author and do not necessarily reflect the views of the publisher, and the publisher hereby disclaims any responsibility for them.

Any people depicted in stock imagery provided by Getty Images are models, and such images are being used for illustrative purposes only.
Certain stock imagery © Getty Images.

ISBN: 978-1-6632-1310-5 (sc)
ISBN: 978-1-6632-1308-2 (hc)
ISBN: 978-1-6632-1309-9 (e)

Library of Congress Control Number: 2020923121

Print information available on the last page.

iUniverse rev. date: 01/13/2021

For our sheepdogs—the hundreds of thousands of police who live out their mission to "protect and serve," especially those who end their watch in the line of duty.

It's possible to assign people to three categories: sheep, wolves, and sheepdogs. Most people fall into the sheep category; they want to go about their business and be left in peace. But that's not always possible. The sheep need protection from the wolves, our predators, who murder, rape, rob, abuse, terrorize, and bully. The sheepdogs live to protect the flock and control wolves; they are our police, soldiers, and other warriors.

—Based upon the book *On Combat* by Lt. Col. Dave Grossman and L. Christensen

Author's Note

My coauthor, Kevin, is my next-door neighbor. He is also a retired police officer and investigator who served for twenty-six years in the Miami-Dade County Police Department.

One day he came to me with about thirty pages of anecdotes—one-page stories about crime scenes in which he directly participated. Each episode was a captivating read. He asked if these incidents could be published, and I explained that, while intriguing, they would be more marketable if they were integrated into a story format. From this discussion, an idea was born: Kevin would tell me his cop stories, and I would write a novel about them.

Quite a challenge. Like most folks, I didn't know a damn thing about the police world. My only conversations with cops stemmed from the few times I was stopped for a traffic violation. I never personally knew a police officer. I am ashamed, too, to admit that I bought into the stereotypical image of a cop as a doughnut-eating gun carrier.

Writing this book has been eye-opening. I had, for example, no awareness of the physical and mental screening it takes these days simply to get accepted as a police candidate. Or of the demanding six-month grind of the police academy (courses ranging from managing medical emergencies to familiarity with state and local laws). Or the requirement to keep current in skills and know-how, such as learning the latest about the identification of autism and the appropriate ways of interacting with those afflicted by it.

So, yes, my attitude about cops has changed. In exploring their world, I learned that they are helpers as much as they are enforcers. They also serve as first responders, rescue workers, detectives, and social workers. Sure, they enforce the law, but in their day-to-day work, much of their effort is directed toward being supportive; most cops try to protect and serve. Their daily patrols make our communities safer places to live.

Lest you believe I have a Pollyannaish view of cops, let me say that I *know* there are hostile cops, corrupt cops, lousy cops, and lazy cops, just as there are in any occupation. But, by and large, your local police are your sheepdogs. They put their lives in jeopardy every time they respond to a robbery or domestic violence, make a traffic stop, or intervene in a bar brawl, to mention only a few risks. On top of it all, they experience the mental stress of seeing the worst of human cruelty, depravity, and disregard for others.

This novel, about a kid desiring to become a cop, will bring you into a world as lived by cops—a world few have seen. After reading it, perhaps you, like me, will view cops with an entirely different perspective.

John D. Drake, PhD

Acknowledgments

Many friends and family members generously provided their time and talent in polishing, editing, and proofreading *New Blue*. Our gratitude to Diane Brewer, James H. K. Bruner, Tim Drake, Carol Ellis, Herman Krone, Frances Losito, Janet Trimper, Tina SoRelle Kozak, and Lieutenant Colonel G.M. "Zak" Kozak, USA Special Forces, Retired. A heartfelt thanks to the Honorable Frank Ledee, Esq., longtime friend and mentor who taught Kevin what a policeman and detective should strive to be.

Much appreciation to Kathy Drake, our proofreader and grammarian extraordinaire.

Our hats off to Dr. Sebastion Milardo and Raymond Inglesi for their insights about the psychological makeup of effective police officers.

A special thanks to John's wife, Delia, who read every revision of this book and made countless suggestions for improving the "read."

If you have provided suggestions and we have messed up and omitted your name, please forgive us. We sincerely appreciate all the help extended to us.

CHAPTER 1

On My Way

My name is Jeremiah Krone, but "Jerry" is what my parents and friends call me. I'm nineteen and think I know everything. But, of course, I don't know much.

In fifth grade, the class bully was a kid named Buzz. It might have been his real name. I'm not sure, but that's what our teacher called him.

One day, just before class began, as we were taking our seats, Buzz pulled the chair out from under me. I went tumbling down amid my classmates' quiet tittering. I felt like an ass, but to add to my distress, Buzz taunted me, as he often did: "Hey, Jerry, does Jerry stand for Geraldine?"

I got so incensed that I stood up and impulsively took a big swing at him. The punch landed on his face. As luck would have it, I hit his nose. Lots of blood. He ended up on the floor, crying. In came the school nurse, who whisked Buzz off to her office, and then the principal took me in tow. You can imagine the hubbub in the classroom.

At the end of the day (I had been returned to the class earlier, after the principal lectured me about fighting), the class watched as Miss Knowles, our teacher, handed me a sealed note for my parents. I knew that I was in big trouble.

When I arrived home, I sheepishly handed the note to my mother. She read it and asked me if I really punched Buzz in the face. I admitted that I did but tried to justify my action by exaggerating a little, saying that he called me a sissy and pulled my chair out. She told me to start my homework and that we'd discuss it more when my father got home. I didn't need a shrink to tell me that she was displeased. Very displeased.

My father was the manager of a Fortuna Beach NAPA Auto Parts store, and it would be a couple of hours before he arrived home. I can remember how anxious and distracted I was. I couldn't even get my English homework done, a subject that was easy for me, wondering all the while what the punishment was going to be. Then I heard the thud of his car door.

When my dad came in the house, my mother handed him the letter. He read it and then asked me, "Is Buzz really the class bully?"

"Yes," I said. "He's always teasing and pushing around us small kids; he pulls the girls' ponytails and takes their hair ribbons. They have to beg him to get them back. It's not right."

My dad then said something that, years later, strongly influenced how I would live my adult life. He told me that bullying was a terrible thing, that what Buzz was doing was wrong. He went on to say, "Jerry, you did the right thing in stopping Buzz. I'm proud of you.

"But I want you to remember something. Violence should never be your first reaction; use it only as a last resort. But if you have to use force, make sure that it's strong enough so that it takes care of the situation. Do you know what I mean?"

"I hear you."

The next day, even before I reached my classroom, six or so of my classmates clamored about me, bubbling with questions: "What did your parents say?" "Did you get punished?" "Are you going to get expelled?" That was the first time I can recall being the center of attention. It was all the more delicious because Amy Stoutmier was among the classmates encircling me. I hadn't yet matured into being interested in girls, but Amy was the most popular girl in our class. I liked her.

The same flurry occurred when I entered the classroom, but along with more questions, I was informed that Buzz had not shown up yet. That information seemed to be conveyed with a certain amount of awe.

As the day proceeded, I grew increasingly aware that most of my classmates approved of my actions and that I was being looked up to. Their words suggested that I was seen as a defender of the smaller kids.

When I reflect on that event today, I see how my father's positive reaction and the approval of my classmates influenced me; their responses helped to shape my values and much of my current mindset.

CHAPTER 2

Now What?

"I've got all right grades, but college doesn't appeal to me," I confessed to Mr. Thornton, the high school guidance counselor. "Not now anyway."

"Why not?" he asked.

"I've been in school all my life. I'm not interested in more schoolwork; I want to get out and do something."

"What would you like to do?"

"That's why I'm meeting with you. I don't know what I would be good at."

"Well, Jerry, let's start with looking at the courses you've taken. Did you find any that were particularly enjoyable or came easily to you?"

"I'm good at math, but I really preferred English Lit."

"Why was that?" he inquired.

"We were asked to analyze what an author meant by a particular phrase or to comment on what the real message of the book was. You had to think beyond the obvious; I was pretty good at that, but I don't know what that means about career choice."

"What do you think about teaching?"

"I could see myself teaching. Actually, I often find myself helping classmates with their homework or prepping for exams. It could be fun, but don't you need a college degree to be a teacher?"

"Yes, you do," Mr. Thornton replied with a hint of optimism crossing his face. "Would the goal of being a teacher change your mind about going to college?"

"Someday it might, but right now I've had enough of school, and I want to see what I can do."

"What do your parents say about what you should do?"

"They are as confused as I am. Neither one of them went to college, and they aren't pushing me to go. Success to them is a steady, well-paying job. They don't talk about careers or finding a job that is really satisfying."

I could see he was frustrated. The poor guy was just trying to do his job, and I wasn't offering up any good leads. Desperation mounting, he tossed out, "In the past year or so, is there anything you did in school that was stimulating, that got your juices flowing?"

I didn't know how to answer. As I thought once more about the classes I had taken, nothing new occurred to me. I already had mentioned the English Lit course. Then it hit me. I remembered something that happened only a week ago.

"Yes, Mr. Thornton, there was something that stirred me. It happened during the midterm exams."

"Tell me about it."

"I saw several classmates cheating. They had crib sheets on their laps or tucked under their shirts. It really got to me. It was so wrong, especially since scores are determined on a curve, and a few answers one way or the other can really change final grades; their cheating could easily influence *my* grade. As I watched them, my blood was boiling. I kept thinking, *It's not right! It's not right!* I wanted to call them out, but of course, I didn't. I just hoped they'd be caught."

"Jerry, have you ever thought about police work?"

CHAPTER 3

January 10

It was a Tuesday evening. My mom, dad, and I were in the middle of dinner; my younger brother, Bob, was with his buddies at a basketball game.

My phone rang.

"Mr. Krone?" A female voice asked.

"Yes."

"I'm calling to tell you that you've been accepted to the Fortuna Beach Police Academy. Are you still interested?"

"Yes, yes, I am!" I exclaimed.

"Well then," she continued, "you should report to the academy on February 1 at 8:00 a.m. I'll be mailing you further information and driving directions. Do you have any questions?"

"No, thank you," I replied. "I'll look forward to receiving the information. Thanks for the call."

I never thought I would hear those words from the academy. I had applied to the FBPD almost a year before—had several interviews, met with their psychologist, took her tests, had a physical exam, and filled out what seemed like countless forms that led to extensive background checks, and now *finally*, I had made it! I slapped the table. With a big smile, I yelled, "Guess what? I got into the academy!"

My dad immediately shouted, "Congratulations! I'm proud of you."

Those were special words; I hadn't heard them often. His expression of pride instantly brought to mind similar words he uttered when I was in the fifth grade. At that time, some nine years ago, neither one of us had any appreciation for how his reaction to my standing up to Buzz—doing the right thing—might have influenced a career choice.

Mom quickly added her "Good for you, Jerry" but with little enthusiasm. She was never a fan of my applying to the academy and often expressed her concerns about the dangers of police work. But her limited support didn't detract from my excitement. We all stood up, hugging one another, savoring the moment.

I could hardly contain myself. I saw the possibilities of a bright future: stable income, pension, and something that was especially important, I would be paid a good salary while attending the academy. I was naively unaware of the downsides, as well of the satisfactions, to be had.

While waiting to hear from FBPD, I had found a job selling cut flowers to retail stores. It was commission only, plus reimbursement for use of my car. Depending on the season, my income varied greatly; some weeks I made a bundle, like during Easter and Thanksgiving. Other times,

I hardly got by. If the police job hadn't come through for me, I wasn't sure where to turn next.

I was impatient to get started; February 1 was only three weeks away, but at that moment, to my nineteen-year-old mind, it seemed like an eternity.

CHAPTER 4

February 1

The morning was clear and cool with temperatures in the fifties; not bad for northern Florida. Dad had already gone to work, but my mom stood on our front steps to wave me off. Despite her trepidations about my becoming a cop, she was smiling. I felt proud as I grabbed my backpack and climbed into my much used and abused '11 Corolla.

I thought that police departments probably functioned like the military, so I decided to be early. That was comfortable for me, ever since I learned about "Lombardi time" from my high school track coach. In sports, arriving fifteen minutes early for practice had served me well.

Driving from our house in Chesterville, a small town that borders Fortuna Beach, I wondered what the academy building and courses would be like. I heard friends describe it as being on a "campus," but somehow my vision of broad lawns and ivy-covered buildings didn't resonate with what I had seen of the Chesterville police building, which was old and not in the greatest of repair.

As I neared the address, I was surprised to find myself entering the gateway for Ocean County Community College.

Following the directions mailed to me, I proceeded along College Avenue, a winding, shaded thoroughfare lined on both sides with old Florida oaks. After about a quarter of a mile, I came to the intersection with Academy Drive, turned left, and saw about a hundred yards ahead a large, two-story redbrick structure cascading with ivy. It looked to be U-shaped and relatively new, with many tall, tinted windows. Behind the building, and a bit to the right, was a large, square patch of asphalt on which were parked four police cars, carefully lined up in a row. I wondered what that was all about.

A nondescript blue-and-white sign declared, "Police Academy." If it weren't for the police cars, I wouldn't have noticed it. I heard that the FBPD and the Ocean County police leased one wing of this classroom building, the other wing being used for regular college classes.

I smiled at the irony; when I was in high school, college wasn't an appealing option, but now, for the next six months, I was going back to school on a college campus.

Entering the building, I was greeted by a uniformed officer who directed me to a large room. Five round tables, with chairs, were placed around the perimeter of the room, and in the center were five rows of desks, six desks to a row. At the front of the classroom were several large whiteboards, a large pull-down projector screen, and a wooden desk with a PC and a sizeable monitor.

As we signed in, we were each given a plastic name tag with our last name embossed on it. We were told to pin it on the right side of our chests and then to sit anywhere we liked. I picked a seat in the second row, away from the action but close enough to be involved, if I wanted to. The name tag of the man next to me read "Scherer." Looking around, I saw that the seats were now filling up. There were about thirty of us.

CHAPTER 5

The Sergeant

At exactly eight o'clock, a sergeant entered the room and stood in front of the now seated class. He was big, over six feet, burly, with a large nose and mouth. Head shaved. Overweight but not fatty looking. He reminded me of Buzz.

"Stand up," he shouted. "When an officer enters the room, you stand up at attention. You should have known that. All up, *now*!

"I'm Sergeant Anton Gagnon," he gruffly told us. "We're going to work your asses off. Get used to it; you don't learn to be a cop by sitting on your tail. I'm going to work you so hard that you'll hate me. The more you hate me, the better I like it.

"To start," he barked, "I want you to count off. We'll begin with you." He pointed to a woman who was standing behind the left-most desk in the first row. "Start!"

She was caught off guard and stuttered for a few seconds before she got out the "One."

"Remember your number. Whenever it's called, you stand at attention. Is that too hard for you recruits? Will you remember your number?"

The class was silent. I think everyone was afraid to speak.

"Well, will you?"

About half the class responded, "Yes, sir."

"Is that as loud as you babies can talk? I thought you were men and women. Baby talk will never get you through this academy. Will you remember your number?"

This time, the answer was loud, almost everyone responding with a crisp, "Yes, sir."

"I don't hear a damn thing. What's the matter with you assholes? Can't you speak a simple answer? Once more, will you *remember*?"

This time, the response was almost ear shattering. The "Yes, sir" shouts echoed off the wooden walls and ceiling.

"You all need more practice. We'll try again later till you get it right."

"Right now, get out your driver's license and Social Security card. I want you to hold them out in front of you. Get them now!"

I felt incredible pressure to hurry. I had the cards in the wallet in my back pocket but had to fumble around to open the pocket button.

I heard some recruit near the back call out, "I don't have them with me."

"You don't have them with you? You mean you drove here without your license? You want to be a cop, and now, before we even get started, you've broken the law! You're toast.

"All right," he shouted. "Where the hell are they? Hold them out in front of you. Let me see them. Okay, starting with number eleven, read off your two numbers. If you don't have your cards, tell us what your numbers are."

Some recruits had their Social Security cards, some didn't. Two recruits didn't have their driver's license. Some knew their SSN by heart; others had no card and no recollection of the number.

The sergeant was ready to explode.

"My God, I've been given a bunch of losers. You're not organized, you break rules, and you don't know a damn thing. You must need some incentive. Everybody down on the floor. Do fifteen push-ups. I want to hear you count off as you do them."

The classroom echoed with murmured moans and groans, except for Scherer, standing next to me. While most of us were frowning, he was smiling, just like he'd been told a funny joke.

The sergeant walked among us, shouting comments like "Let's hear it," and "Don't give up, sissy, or you'll be starting all over again."

"What kind of bullshit is this!" came a voice from a couple of rows behind me.

The sergeant immediately turned and faced the challenger, his face livid. He spewed, "If you can't take the heat, you don't belong here. Make up your mind right now, kid. This is nothing compared to what lies ahead."

"That's an easy decision," the recruit shouted back. "I've had enough of this crap." Without another word, he left the classroom.

That recruit was right, I thought. *What kind of shit is this? Terrible. He got put down for reacting like a human being. At least he had the guts to speak up.*

My nineteen years of a rather sheltered life left me totally unprepared for the sergeant's harassment. I felt torn. My anger was urging me to say, "I'm leaving too." But my yearlong wait to get in the academy made me hesitate. I didn't want to blow the opportunity to be a cop on my first day there.

As I was completing my eleventh push-up, Scherer, supporting himself with only his right arm, reached over with his left and touched my forearm, his way of signaling to me to cool it.

The sergeant continued ranting, "This is the worst class I've ever been assigned to. We'll be lucky if half of you make it." With that comment, he threw an empty chair, sending it skidding across the front of the room. He then left, going out the door he had come in.

CHAPTER 6

Anger

Another sergeant entered the classroom.

"Ten ... tion," he commanded.

Everyone in my line of vision, including myself, stood straight and tall.

"At ease," he said. "Be seated. I'm Sergeant Drominskey."

A palpable calm came over the room. It amazed me. He was a sergeant like Gagnon, but he exuded a relaxed confidence that commanded respect. He didn't upset and annoy me. The atmosphere in the classroom was like the proverbial calm after the storm.

"Listen, recruits," he began, "everything we do here has a purpose, even though you may not see that purpose. We expect you to get angry about what we make you do. We do it for a reason. We're going to mold you. We're going to mold you to become effective cops. You're going to have to leave your old life—your civilian life—behind.

"At the academy, you're going to feel a lot of heat because, on the job, you're going to have to take a lot of heat. Do what we command, and you'll be able to handle it."

This was a more reasoned way of teaching, I thought. I laughed to myself. *Did I just experience a good cop/bad cop routine?*

"Now, let's get back to work. It's important for everyone to learn their numbers, and right now, every recruit also needs to memorize their Social Security and driver's license numbers. Since many of you don't have that information. We want you to get it.

"We're going to take a fifteen-minute break to give you time to go to your car, make some phone calls—whatever it takes—but get those numbers. If you have time left before the break is up, use it to start memorizing them."

Since I had my two cards, I started to memorize the numbers. The Social Security card was easy—a three-two-four sequence; the driver's license was harder, having an odd combination of letters and numbers.

At that moment, Scherer turned toward me. "Hi, I'm Don Scherer."

"Man," I responded, "I never expected anything like this. My name is Jerry Krone."

Sergeant Drominskey then called us to attention. We all stood.

"When I call your number, read to me, as loudly as you can, your driver's license and Social Security numbers." Those who couldn't provide both numbers were humiliated by the sergeant's criticism and his urging "to get with it," but it was said with less abusiveness than Sergeant Gagnon.

We were then told to be ready to recite both card numbers, by heart, during tomorrow's class. Homework already.

After lunch, the sergeant appointed five squad leaders. He explained that these leaders were all ex-military and that their responsibility was to be sure that all members of their squad succeeded in the academy. "Not only succeed," he said, "but excel."

I was happy to learn that I was assigned to Don's squad. He, unlike Sergeant Gagnon, seemed mature and someone I could respect. Each of the squads then moved to an assigned table where we introduced ourselves and shared why we had decided to apply to the academy. An interesting session.

About three o'clock, Sergeant Gagnon reentered the classroom. He boomed, "Ten … tion," and then proceeded to shout. "Now, all you fat-ass, slow, and ill-conditioned creatures, we're going to start getting you whipped into shape.

"In your acceptance letter, you were told to bring with you running shoes and gym clothes. You have ten minutes to change and to get back here at your desk."

"I don't have any running shoes," some recruit cried out from behind me.

"Tough shit," the sergeant barked back. "You were told to bring them. If you can't follow directions, run in what you have. This isn't some nursery school, kid. Get with it."

A motley-looking group returned from changing in the bathrooms: some wore gym shorts, some surfer pants, some sweatpants, some T-shirts, and some sports bras overlayered by something that looked like a man's undershirt—all in all a ragtag-looking group.

I thought the sergeant would make snide remarks about the appearance of his class, but instead he shouted, "When I blow this whistle, each squad leader is to take his squad to the track and run two laps, then touch the wall at the obstacle course, and get back to this room as fast as you can. You're not back until every last member of your squad is back. The squad that gets here last gets to do a ton of push-ups. If you don't know where the track is, find it."

More bullshit, I thought. But Don didn't give me time to nurse my anger. He quickly said, "Okay, gang, let's do the best we can. It will help if we stick together and encourage each other. I'll lead the way, and everyone try to stay close to me."

The whistle blew for us to start running.

Our squad came back first! Sweaty and exhausted, but there were high fives all around. For the first time that day, I smiled. I was proud of our squad.

At four o'clock, just before we were dismissed, we were informed that tomorrow was "uniform day." We were told to pick up our uniforms at the quartermaster's office in the Fortuna Police Building at any time after 0800 hours and to be back in the classroom, in full uniform, no later than 1000 hours.

On the drive home, I had a jumble of feelings: anger at Sergeant Gagnon's teaching methods and, at the same time, worry about the possibility of overreacting to his shenanigans. Yet, intermingled with those feelings was a sense of satisfaction about how our squad encouraged and helped one another, especially those who were tiring or lagging. Even though we were joined together for only one event, it seemed that we were on our way to becoming a team.

Though I was feeling wiped out, I decided to put my concerns aside and wait to see what tomorrow would bring.

CHAPTER 7

Tyler

Two years ago, about the time Jerry was beginning his senior year at Chesterville High, someone unknown to him was starting eighth grade at Fortuna Beach Junior High. His name was Tyler. He was barely thirteen; his body was thin, and to his frustration, the bathroom scale seemed stuck on eighty-five. He wondered if he'd ever get to be more like some kids who looked cool and were popular.

It also was disturbing when he caught glimpses of other boys in the locker room; he was becoming increasingly conscious of the fact that, unlike some of his classmates, nothing much was happening between his legs. He had no hair, and his "wee-wee" (a term his mother still used, much to his embarrassment) was nowhere near anything he was going to parade around.

During that school year (eighth grade), he also became aware that his dick—that's what his school buddies called it—might be more than a tool for urinating, that it could produce pleasant, tingly feelings.

The first experience of these vibes occurred one afternoon when he arrived home from school later than

27

usual. Sally, his older sister, sixteen, wearing only her bra and panties, was walking along the upstairs corridor, on her way to the bathroom for a shower. As chance would have it, Tyler was quietly coming up the stairs—shoes off, obeying his mother's rule to prevent soiling the carpeting. It was essential to obey her rules, or else he knew he'd feel her hairbrush on his bottom. It didn't happen often these days, but he got plenty of smacks when he was younger.

At the moment Tyler's head and shoulders cleared the top step, directly in front of him, a few yards away, was his sister. Tyler had seen her around the house in her underwear plenty of times and thought nothing of it. Today, something was different. His eyes darted to pink lace, and as he looked, he saw through the thin fabric a dark patch at her crotch and some black curls peeking out from under the panties. The sight was intriguing; it struck him as something forbidden, sort of mysterious and naughty. Spontaneously, his little penis stood up straight, and in his groin, he felt a warm, pleasant glow. This was something entirely new to Tyler.

Sally responded to the encounter with relative calm—after all, it was just her kid brother—expressing surprise that he was in the house but then continuing on to the bathroom. She was not at all cognizant of Tyler's sexual arousal.

Tyler was surprised by his body's reaction, and he thought he'd like to feel like that again. Maybe, he mused, it could be recaptured by touching her panties. To that end, he waited for an opportunity, and one afternoon when the house was empty, he entered his sister's bedroom. The room was a mess—shoes and clothes strewn about and hanging haphazardly off her chair—but no underwear.

Moving to her dresser, Taylor began opening drawers. In the top drawer, on the right, he found what he was looking for: at least a dozen panties—many white, one black, and six or more pink. When he reached down and touched one of the pink ones, he experienced some of the warm, tingling sensations as when he had spotted his sister in the hallway.

He decided not to steal them, knowing he could come back anytime his sister wasn't home.

That afternoon marked the beginning of a new phase in Tyler's development.

CHAPTER 8

A Man in Blue

"Thirty-four," the quartermaster boringly intoned as he measured my arm length. What a surprise! The last time I was measured, it was for a jacket for the freshmen prom. At that time, a thirty-inch sleeve was a perfect fit. I had a growth spurt in my sophomore and junior years but didn't realize how much I'd changed. Once a scrawny kid, I was turning out to be like my mom—tall with long legs that helped me to become a varsity high school quarter-miler. But I wasn't skinny. I inherited my father's broad shoulders and chest.

As I donned the light blue recruit uniform in the police locker room, I felt strange vibes, sort of like an energy surge. It struck me that this was a special moment. While buttoning the shirt with the Fortuna Beach Police insignia on the right sleeve, I noticed that I was standing tall. I sensed that I had just taken a big step and was feeling proud.

Returning to the classroom at about nine thirty, I found two stapled sheets of paper on my desk. At the top of the first sheet, the word "CONFIDENTIAL" appeared in bold red ink. The next line read, "FBPD Radio Signals." A quick glance revealed nearly a hundred signals, each designated by a number. Scanning the list, I noted that Signal "1" was "Drunk Driver," "10" was "Stolen Vehicle", and "34" was "Officer Calling for Help." That one stopped me. Immediately, my mind jumped to an image of my mother warning me about the dangers of police work. "It's not good when you have to deal with criminals all the time," was a phrase she often uttered.

"Ten … tion!" jolted me out of my reverie. It was Sergeant Gagnon. When I looked up, his eyes were squinting, and his mouth formed an angry-looking, inverted U shape.

"Let's see if you idiots have learned anything," he shouted. "Number twenty-five, we'll start with you. Tell me your social security and your driver's license number. Don't read them to me; you should know them by heart."

And so it went, much like the day before. If you knew your numbers, and all but two of us did, he said nothing. Not a word of praise or acknowledgment. But for the two who missed even one number, all hell broke loose. He condemned their laziness, stupidity, and lack of motivation and then shouted, "You must need more incentive. Twenty push-ups should get you motivated. Do them right now by your desk. And before you leave today, you recite your numbers to me. Now get to work."

I felt anger rise to the surface. One of the recruits apparently had worked to memorize his two sets of numbers and only stumbled over the last couple of digits on his driver's license. He seemed to be nervous and was struggling to come up with the right numbers when the sergeant jumped in and cut him off before he could regroup. I felt sorry for the recruit and tensed, ready to stand up and do battle. I wanted to yell, "Give him a chance! He's getting it!" I was beginning to hate Sergeant Gagnon.

The sergeant then picked up his copy of the radio signals. Waving them in the air, he loudly proclaimed, "These signals and code numbers are one of the most important things you will learn at the academy. You will memorize every fucking one of these signals. You will be tested over and over again. You will have until your weeklong riding assignment to learn every last one of them. That will be about three months from now. If you don't know all the signals, no riding assignment. No riding assignment, no graduation. Is that clear?"

The "Yes, sirs" were loud. Despite our dislike for the sergeant, we were learning.

"Is that clear?"

The "Yes, sirs!" thundered across the classroom.

CHAPTER 9

Don's Advice

At lunch break, as we were standing to leave for the cafeteria, Don asked, "Do you want to join me for lunch?"

"Yes, thank you," I said. I was flattered that our squad leader wanted to be with me. I was young enough to be his son and never would have had the balls to ask him to lunch. Similar to Gagnon, he was tall, over six feet, broad shoulders, with a scruffy salt and pepper beard, thinning hair, and a large, square-jawed face. He walked and sat with his back straight, like many in military service. In fact, one of the older recruits, John Hoffmann, told me that Don had "extensive combat experience." Physically, Don was intimidating, yet he had a warm, engaging personality.

Once we filled our trays and found a table, we chatted for a few minutes about the cafeteria food (as bad as you might guess), and then Don asked me, "How strongly do you want to be a cop?"

I jerked up my head. I was startled and uncertain how to answer. Considering that we hardly knew each other, it struck me as being too personal a question. But I didn't take it as an idle comment either; he seemed genuinely interested in me.

"Don, I weighed a lot of options, and this one, being a cop, seemed just right. Frankly, if I don't make it at the academy, I wouldn't know where to head next."

"Okay," Don replied, "the reason I asked is that you seemed quite upset and angry at the way Sergeant Gagnon handled the class. At one point there, I thought you might leave like the other recruit did."

"I almost walked out, but I didn't want to give up on the first day of class. Oh, and thank you for encouraging me to cool down."

"Can I offer you a little advice?"

"Sure."

"I've been in the army for the past twenty years. Just recently retired. But during my army career, I ran into many drill sergeants like Gagnon. He has a tough job. He's charged with taking a hodge-podge collection of people—all with different expectations, different ethnic and family backgrounds, different attitudes, and a hell of a lot of other differences—and molding them to be alike in many ways. Molding them to be cops. He has to do that because life as a cop, like the army, is entirely different than civilian life."

"Well," I responded, "it seems like a hell of a way to do it. Why does he scream and rant and throw chairs and make us do push-ups for stupid shit like a driver's license number? To me, it gets in the way of learning."

"Jerry, I have found it helpful to think that there is a lesson in almost everything the instructors do. They are trying to prepare us for police work. You can't do that with only textbooks and lectures because you also need to learn to cope with hostility, pressure, stress, put-downs and spit-in-your-face behavior. You learn *that* kind of stuff by actually dealing with it. That's what's happening in the classroom."

"Well, I don't think that doing push-ups teaches me anything about being a cop."

"But the funny thing is that the push-ups are a lesson too. They help strengthen your upper body. That's important not only for battling with perps who might attack you but also for holding your gun steady. In about five weeks. We'll be spending a lot of time on the firing range. If you don't have a strong upper body, you won't be able to support the weight of your pistol as you try to hold it out in front of you. If it's like the army, you'll need to be able to do that hour after hour. And I do know this: if you don't qualify on the range, you don't graduate.

"Remember the squad that came in last from running the laps? They all had to do ten extra push-ups, and you were pissed off at Gagnon. But that squad includes the frailest guy in our class and two women. The added body conditioning will help them on the range and on the job."

Somewhat humbled, I said, "I never thought of it that way."

"Jerry, I think you'll make a good cop, and the academy is a great place to learn to be one. Just don't get caught up in the instructor's delivery. When I was in the army, I learned to look past the presentation and ask myself, 'What is the lesson being taught? What can I learn from what is going on?' Maybe you'll find that mindset helpful too."

I wasn't totally convinced, but I wanted to be a cop, and I could see that I was fighting the actions they were using that could, eventually, help me.

As we picked up our trays, I said, "Don, thanks for the advice. I appreciate your thoughts, and I'll give them a whirl."

CHAPTER 10

Close Call

Six months had elapsed since Tyler's sexual awakening, and this morning he noticed a peach-like fuzz beginning to emerge in his armpits and near his dick. Things were finally happening.

Another significant event took place at about the same time. It occurred in the Fortuna Beach's Central Park. "Central," as everyone called it, was about a half mile from Tyler's house. It was the town's largest park with a couple of Little League baseball fields, swings, seesaws, plastic house-like structures for climbing on, a couple of tennis courts, and an obstacle course. The course was designed for kids, but it was challenging for any young adult, like Tyler, who tried to conquer it at a fast pace.

Tyler wasn't much into team sports. His father died when he was an infant, and he was raised by his mother. She wasn't very athletic, so unlike his classmates' fathers, who played catch or tossed a football to their sons, she never encouraged him to practice sports or to join a team. She seemed to drink a lot and was usually too busy doing girlie things with his sister.

On this particular day, while Tyler was sitting on a park bench, resting after his obstacle course run, he noticed that one of the backyards bordering the park had a long clothesline. On it were shirts, socks, shorts, and a pair of pink panties! He felt a slight tingle and thought that it might be stronger if he could touch and fondle them. He was surprised that the urge was so strong. As he sat there, he couldn't stop thinking about the panties and what they might do for him. He decided to get them.

Tyler figured that if he waited for nighttime to try to snatch them, they might be gone from the line. Besides, he couldn't think of a good excuse to go there after dark. He realized it was now or never but wasn't sure how he could get to them. A wire mesh fence, about as high as his shoulders, encircled the park and kept the backyard inaccessible. He needed an excuse to get on the other side of the fence.

Tyler had an idea. He would need a ball but puzzled over where he could find one. He thought about the tennis courts, wondering if one could be found in the courtside trash cans. Fortunately, he didn't have to dig around in the trash because right there, on one court, lying in a corner, was a faded yellow ball. It hardly had any bounce, but that wasn't a problem. He picked it up, walked back to the yard, and tossed the ball over the fence toward a spot near the undies.

He went to the end of the fence (at the entrance gate) and walked along the outside of it until he came to the yard. Pausing to check if anyone was looking, he casually strolled to the ball, picked it up with his left hand, and then quickly, with his right, pulled the two panties off the line and stuffed them into his pocket.

Tyler heard a woman yell, "Hey, kid. What are you doing here?"

He quickly turned toward the sound of the shout and saw, standing in her doorway, an attractive woman about his mother's age. She was short and blondish and wore floral-patterned shorts with a blue T-shirt.

Tyler panicked. One of his worst fears came true: he had been caught. Thoughts raced through his mind: *How am I going to get out of this? How could I ever explain this to my mother?* If she was drinking when she found out, his buttocks would be sore for a week. He wished for the magical power to become invisible. *What am I going to say to this lady?*

Tyler thought of the ball in his hand. He held it up high to show the woman and said, "My ball got tossed over the fence. I just came in to get it."

"This is private property; you shouldn't be in my yard. Come over here."

Tyler didn't think for a second more; he turned and ran. As he was escaping, the woman shouted, "I'm going to call the police!"

Tyler ran as fast as his adrenaline-fed legs could move. When he reached Central's parking lot, he was gasping for breath, but he kept on running all the way home.

CHAPTER 11

Success and Humility

On the day following Don's counseling, I decided to see if his advice would work.

I made an effort to look past the sergeants' orders and methods of delivery and instead focus on what they were trying to teach us. The change was incredibly helpful; their antics still ruffled me but not anywhere near as much as before. To my surprise, I occasionally smiled, even when we had to do push-ups!

Then, another good thing happened. It was Thursday afternoon of week three, and Sergeant Drominskey said, "Listen up. Sometime this Friday, Saturday, or Sunday, you will be assigned to ride in a patrol car. For one entire shift, you will ride with a patrol officer to see how things are handled on the job. You're going to find out what it's like to be a cop.

"Make sure you bring your notepad and flashlight with you. Between now and your riding assignment, learn more radio signals. If you don't, you're going to feel stupid when your training officer asks you what a signal means. We've taught you a lot about police tactics already. Don't do anything stupid, and respond immediately to your training officer's directions.

"I have given each squad leader a list of all riding assignments. When you're dismissed, ask your squad leader the day and hour of your shift."

Don told me that I was assigned to the HQ station for the 2-10 shift on Saturday afternoon. The only comment he added was "Get there twenty minutes early."

I had a Saturday-night movie date with Janet, my current throb, and thought about asking for a different assignment time. However, I quickly rejected the idea, imagining how Sergeant Gagnon would react to such a request.

The class was abuzz with excitement—our first venture out of the classroom, the real thing. All of us began comparing notes: "What shift did you get?" "Hey, look at this: we're both on tonight!" I remember hoping that my patrol assignment would be filled with action. I didn't realize what I was asking for.

CHAPTER 12

The Ride

Following both Don's advice and the *Lombardi time* principle, I arrived at the HQ police station twenty minutes before two. When I opened the main door, I was confronted with a huge lobby, maybe thirty feet wide, with broad hallways leading off to the left and right. An elevator was in the center.

I felt excited about getting exposed to real cop work but also was a little overwhelmed, like the first day at a new school. A gray-haired woman, seated behind the counter, was staring intently at her computer. "I'm here for a ride-along today. Can you tell me where the roll call room is?"

Without looking up or greeting me, she said, "Down the corridor to your right. It's at the end."

So much for a warm welcome. The toughening-up process never seemed to cease.

Entering the roll call room, my academy uniform clearly revealed me as an outsider. I looked like some college kid—no gun, no badge. I stood as tall as I could and, with a look of confidence, walked into the room. It was like a small classroom, with rows of tables that served as desks. Two officers were seated at the tables, one looking at notes and the other reading a newspaper; three others were chattering away near a table that held the coffee pot.

Standing in the back of the room, by herself, was another recruit, Bridget. She looked as though she was feeling the same as me—out of place and unwanted.

As I began walking toward her, she spotted me and broke into a warm smile. I melted. Bridge, as she was called, was very attractive. Her dark black hair provided a striking contrast to her fair Irish skin. Nice figure. She looked sturdy, not like someone you could easily push around.

"Hi, Bridge," I called. "Glad to see you."

"Same here. Not a very friendly place, is it?"

"Maybe it's all part of the toughening process, like the stuff Sergeant Gagnon lays on us."

Just then, two more recruits—Tony and Rico—entered the room and walked toward us. As they passed the coffee-drinking police officer group, I heard one say, "Sure looks like we're down to the bottom of the barrel."

I experienced instant ire. *What makes him think he's so damn superior?* But, remembering Don's advice, I canned the anger almost as quickly as it came.

At that moment, the sergeant bellowed, "Let's go," and with that, everyone seated themselves. The four of us recruits found some empty seats in the last row.

After the roll call and seemingly endless announcements, the sergeant, whose name tag read "Gallagher," said, "We

46

have four riding assignments today." He then read off the officer/recruit pairings.

"Stay safe out there," Gallagher said, and the roll call broke up. From the front table emerged an officer who looked fit and trim, about thirty, with slightly darkened skin and black hair. He strode toward the four of us and asked, "Who is Jerry Krone?"

"Me," I proudly stated.

Extending his hand, he said, "Jerry, I'm Jose Rodriquez. We'll be riding together. Welcome to the world of the Fortuna Beach Police."

As Jose and I departed, I turned to our little group of recruits and said, "Good luck, guys ... and Bridge. See you Monday."

Tony and Rico mumbled their "good lucks," but Bridge said, "Knock 'em dead, Jerry. Well, er, not really. You know what I mean. I'll look forward to hearing how it goes for you."

"Okaaaay," I said, surprised that it came out with such enthusiasm.

CHAPTER 13

Patrol Car

On our way to the patrol car, we stopped by the gun racks, and Jose handed me two shotguns to tote. A rookie chore, I supposed.

Once at the car, Jose asked, "Have you had experience with shotguns?"

"No," I said. "I'm familiar with a twenty-two rifle but not with a shotgun."

"All right," he said. "You'll get shotgun training when you go to the range. But for now, I want you to be able to defend yourself *and me.*"

He placed the shotguns on the top of the trunk, explaining that the black one was to be used as a deadly force, the shells filled with heavy buckshot. The other, orange colored, had a less lethal load that would stop someone but not kill them. He said, "You don't have to aim the shotgun like a rifle, because when you fire, the pellets scatter, and the possibility of missing is slight. Just point at the target and pull the trigger."

Next, Jose had me practice loading and reloading until I could do it quickly and smoothly. He then placed the nonlethal shotgun in the trunk, and while the lid was open, he pointed out other vital trunk items: first aid kit, flares, emergency blanket, traffic cones, camera, and evidence bags.

Carrying the black shotgun, Jose asked me to come around with him to the driver's door. He had me practice taking the unloaded shotgun in and out of an overhead rack until I could quickly remove the gun. With that done, Jose loaded the gun and locked it in the rack.

"Jerry, we have no idea what we'll run into on patrol. Hopefully, we won't need the shotguns, but we could find ourselves in a situation where either one of us is trapped or in danger. I have a young family; I want to go home tonight. I need you to be able to cover me."

"I'll do everything I can."

"Good," Jose replied. "The most important thing you can do is get help if we need it. I want you to be able to use our radio to call for backup without a second's hesitation. So, before we pull out of the station, we're going to get you comfortable with using it. Okay?"

"Yes, sir. I want to learn."

When I entered the car on the passenger side, the first thing that struck me was the odor. "Phew!" I loudly reacted.

"What's the matter?" Jose inquired.

"What's the matter?" I said. "Don't you smell that?"

"I don't smell anything," he said in a surprised tone. Then, after a long pause, his broad smile revealed bright white teeth. "Just jerking your chain, Jerry. All patrol cars smell. It's the perfume of police work. Get in, and I'll tell you about it.

"You better get used to the stink because from now on, the patrol car is going to be your office, and you'll be in your office every day you're on the job." He explained that the smell came from fast foods, coffee, urine, vomit, alcohol, blood, sweat, and fear—mostly from perps—who had been placed in the rear seats. "We have to clean it, but that just adds a chemical smell to the mix. It's almost impossible to eliminate all the stink."

For the next five minutes, we reviewed and practiced the simple procedure of using the handheld mic and reciting, over and over again, the call for backup. I learned that we were unit 1312 and that the radio signal for help was "10-34."

"Jerry, you don't need to remember this for today, but it could be helpful to understand how radio call signs are designed—they're not just random numbers.

"Take, for example our unit number, 1312. The first digit is always the district. The one we have means that we're operating out of the HQ district; we'd begin with a two if we were in the western district. The second number tells the shift we're on. The three we have stands for afternoon shift; one would be for midnight and two for the day shift. The third digit, the one, represents the zone we're patrolling. Each district has two zones, and we've been given—as you have probably already figured out—zone one. Our fourth number tells about squad seniority. Since

I'm the second most senior officer working this afternoon, a two was assigned to our unit number. And so, Jerry, that's how we ended up being 1312."

Nodding slowly, I murmured, "Uh huh."

Jose must have thought I was confused, because he went on to explain, "Jerry, I know all this may seem complicated, but it really keeps radio traffic chaos to a minimum. You'll quickly learn what unit is getting a call and approximately where they are. Remember, at any given time, there are twelve to fifteen units on the radio. The unit numbering system helps the dispatcher keep things straight. Your life may depend upon that."

Jose then handed me a marking pen. "I want you to write our unit number on the back of your hand. It's washable."

"I'll remember it," I protested.

"In a crisis situation, you may or may not remember. Write it now."

I said, "Okay," but I hated being treated as a child. I'm sure Jose detected my reluctance

"Jerry, writing our unit number on your hand may seem unnecessary, but it's not. I know of an incident when doing that saved a life. A few years back, an officer was shot in the mouth while checking a car that had a rape in progress. He couldn't speak. He shot the rapist, grabbed the victim, held the radio, and pointed to his hand that had his unit number on it; he keyed the mic so the victim could broadcast the number. When the dispatcher heard the message, she had some idea where the officer was, and she set up a search pattern. The dispatcher saved his life.

"What's our unit, Jerry?"

"One-three-one-two."

"Good. Now, when we get out there, I want you to be aware, at all times, of exactly where we are—what street we're on, what corner we're at, what direction we're going in, or the address we're at. Try to remember *O-N-E—odd* numbers are on the *north* and *east* sides. Help will come quickest when everyone knows exactly where we are. Questions?"

"No, sir." I was starting to feel a bit overwhelmed, and we hadn't even left the parking lot. At the same time, I couldn't wait for us to get moving out on patrol.

"Just a few more items," Jose said. "For your safety and mine, you need to follow my directions quickly, without hesitation. Consider them an order. If you have a question or an issue, do what I tell you first, then ask me later. I want you to learn, but I want both of us to return healthy at the end of the shift.

"Reality begins when we drive out of the gate. Bad shit happens, *fast*. Keep your head on a swivel. If I get hurt, you better be in the hospital bed next to me!

"Most of the time, you will be able to accompany me out of the car, but when I tell you to stay, *stay!* Be alert to what is happening and be ready to make that backup call."

"Suppose I see some danger, like someone going to attack you, but you don't know they are there."

"By all means, get my attention. But get help too! You'll have to rely on your best judgment. Keep in mind, safety is number one. If harm can be avoided, don't put you or me at risk."

I had envisioned the day as an interesting ride in a patrol car, but there we were, talking about life-and-death issues.

"So, what do you think, Jerry? Are you ready for your riding assignment?"

"Is any recruit ever ready? I'll do my best. Let's go."

Jose picked up the radio transmitter and said, "One-three-one-two, ten-eight with a trainee."

"Ten-four, one-three-one two."

With that, we rolled out of the HQ parking lot.

CHAPTER 14

The Fence

It was a sunny Saturday afternoon almost a year since Tyler's stair-top encounter with his sister. The house was empty, and he was heading to the garage for his bike when he came to the upstairs hallway window. He looked out to see if there were any storm clouds, and as he did, his eye caught a woman reading a book in the next yard. She was stretched out on a lounge chair wearing a skimpy white bikini.

Until today, women had not been an attraction for Tyler, but now, to his astonishment, he didn't want to take his eyes from the scene. He noticed that her breasts almost entirely spilled out of her bikini top and that he could also see her crotch. But, unlike his sister, no hairs were evident. Still, he felt the beginning of that tingly sensation. He liked it and wanted more.

He thought that if he were closer to the woman, he could get an even better view, maybe more thrill. While he never paid much attention to the tall fence that marked the end of his backyard, he knew that it was in ill repair and close to falling down; worth checking out.

As Tyler approached the fence, it was clear that there were many open spaces between the boards. Cautiously, he neared one small slit and peered through. There she was, on her patio, only thirty feet away. *This is wrong*, he thought. *I'm spying. I should stop.* Yet he was reluctant to take his eyes off the woman because his dick became hard, and it felt good.

Hardly a day passed without Tyler stopping at the second-floor hallway window, but only twice in the past six months did he see the bikinied lady. On those occasions, he concocted an excuse to go out in the yard, but that didn't reduce the uneasiness he felt, knowing that he could be seen by at least one of the next-door neighbors—Mr. McPherson, the grouchy old man in the yellow house to the right. It was even harder to conjure a good reason for peeking through the fence; he knew that his spying had to be fleeting.

Each time he peeked at the woman through the fence, it was accompanied by a desire to touch her panties. After the second observation, the urge became stronger, strong enough that he envisioned stealing a pair; it led to his daydreaming about sneaking into her bedroom.

Tyler decided to make a plan.

CHAPTER 15

The Ticket

Once I buckled my patrol car seat belt, I felt hemmed in, almost claustrophobic. Jose's radio and computer encroached into the passenger's space, and all around the dashboard and windshield frame were handcuffs, switches, buttons, levers, and God knows what. It looked like an airliner cockpit.

We began our patrol by cruising down Ocean Boulevard, a busy four-lane street lined on both sides with drugstores, car dealerships, fast-food restaurants, gas stations, and small shopping malls.

It didn't take long for action to begin.

Up ahead, Jose spotted a green Ford coming out of a side street. The driver slid right into the intersection, ignoring a stop sign.

"Listen up, Jerry," Jose commanded. "Sometime during our ride, I was going to let you observe a traffic stop, but now we've got one right away."

Jose hit the flashing lights switch, and off we went. My heart started beating faster.

The driver must have seen the patrol car's lights, and slowly pulled off the boulevard into a CVS parking lot.

"Your job," said Jose, "will be to observe and make sure we're safe. When we're parked and I go to the stopped car, you will get out of this car and stand by the open door on your side. I want you to have access to the radio. Stay there unless I get hurt or I ask you to come to me. If I call you, I will tell you what side of the car to go to."

"Yes, sir. Oh, look!" I shouted, interrupting Jose and pointing toward the car we pulled over. "One of the taillights doesn't work."

"Good observation, Jerry. The thing to remember about stops is that for the most part they are routine, possibly the only dialogue some people will ever have with a cop. But they are also one of the most dangerous events you will encounter. And, don't forget, know where you are at all times. Where are we, Jerry?"

Thank God I had looked around when we stopped. "We're on Ocean Boulevard and Eighteenth Street," I proudly proclaimed.

"What's the number on the building?"

"I don't know."

"You should know. Always look around for ways to pinpoint your location. The more specific you are, the quicker help can arrive. This is important, Jerry. Your life and your partner's may depend on it."

Jose radioed, "One-three-one-two, ten-fifty at 11458 Ocean Boulevard, CVS parking lot."

The dispatcher responded, "One-three-one-two at 11458 Ocean Boulevard, CVS parking lot."

Jose then left the patrol car (we were about a car's length behind the Ford). I was eager to see how this potentially dangerous encounter was done, so I studiously watched each step he took. He stopped just behind the driver's side doorpost so that the driver had to look over his or her shoulder to see him. Jose spoke a while with the driver and then returned.

When we were both back inside the patrol car, Jose explained, "I advised the driver, a woman of about thirty, that I pulled her over for failing to stop at a stop sign. Then I asked her for her driver's license, registration, and insurance card. She told me that she left her wallet at home with the DL, but she produced the two other cards. The car is registered in her name. So, now we'll run her DL and check if there are any warrants. When the dispatcher calls back, I want you to be ready to write down the information she gives us."

When the radio check came in, the dispatcher reported that the DL was valid and that she had no ticket history.

"All right, Jerry, what do we have here? How many violations?"

"Well," I said, "that's easy. Three. She ran a stop sign, didn't have her driver's license, and she has a brake light that's not working."

"Right on," said Jose. "What would you write her for?"

CHAPTER 16

What's Right?

"Well, three violations, three tickets. That's the law. Am I missing something here?"

"I think you might be," Jose said. "How much are the tickets?"

"I don't know."

"Ah, I see. You should learn the common fines. Here's what we have: For the DL, she can go to court, show her license, and just pay court costs of fifty dollars. Of course, this takes time away from work. Or she can pay a hundred and twenty-five dollars for a nonmoving violation.

"The stop sign is a moving violation—a hundred and seventy-five bucks plus some points on her license. Again, she can go to court and that takes time. For the brake light, she could pay a hundred-and-twenty-five-dollar fine or she could get it fixed and have a cop sign off on the repair, five dollars."

I thought to myself, *Why is he telling me about the fines?* Was I expected to know them? "Is there a problem?" I asked.

"Jerry, I want you to look at the car. What do you see?"

"Well, it's a Ford, maybe ten years old. A little beat up. I'm not sure what the model is. Looking through the back window, I can see a car seat."

"Right now, I'm writing a citation for the brake light. When I'm finished, we'll go up to her car. You come up to the passenger side while I go to the driver's side and hand her the ticket."

When we arrived at the car, the first thing Jose said to the driver was, "Do you mind my asking what you do for a living?"

"I work at Walmart," said the woman, her cheeks wet with tears.

"Thank you," Jose said. "You committed three traffic violations: running a stop sign, failing to exhibit your driver's license on demand, and one brake light is out. But I see that you have been driving for nine years and you've never had a ticket. So, I've only written you a citation for the brake light. Get it fixed. I'm sure one of the mechanics in the tire department at Walmart can do it for you. Then find a cop and have him sign the ticket, proving it was fixed. It's a five-dollar fine; send it in with the envelope I'm giving you; the instructions are right there. You can go to court if you wish, and the instructions also tell you about that."

The woman's shoulders slumped as her tension dissipated. "Oh, thank you so much, Officer. I'll be more careful."

Walking back to the patrol car, Jose asked, "Why didn't I write three tickets as you recommended?"

"It might have been a hardship."

"Continue," said Jose.

"Well, she probably doesn't make that much, and she has a baby."

"But," said Jose, "she committed three offenses."

"Yes," I said, as dawn broke. "You've got to use good judgment too. What's right is right, but right isn't always what you think right is."

"You're learning. She had three violations. But here's the reality: she works at Walmart, making maybe twelve dollars an hour, and she has a child. Let's say she works a forty-hour week. That's four hundred and eighty dollars, maybe three fifty after taxes. If she goes to court, she'll lose a day's pay and fifty dollars.

"If she pays the fine because she can't get off from work, its over three hundred dollars, even if she takes care of the stoplight. So, little or no money for a week. Another thing to remember, Jerry, is that she has a clean driving record. If you ticket the moving violation, her insurance may increase—another hit on her income. The likely outcome is ill will.

"It's not always wise to crush someone. None of us is perfect. How many of your classmates didn't have their Social Security cards and DLs on your first day at the academy?

"Okay," Jose said, "Let's wrap things up. What do you see as the purpose of making traffic stops?"

I so wanted to come up with the right answer; knowing I was being tested, I didn't want to fail. I took a long few seconds. And finally, remembering something I learned at the academy, I answered, "To enforce the laws. To try and prevent accidents and traffic chaos."

"Good answer. If we gave her the three tickets, would she be more conscientious about future violations than if we just gave her one?"

"No, she'd probably be upset, maybe feel resentful, believing that she was punished too harshly."

"Good. Do you think our lady will be more careful in the future?"

"Yes."

I thought, *If I don't get involved with any more police situations today, it's okay; I've already learned a lot.*

CHAPTER 17

A Door

It had been a while since Tyler had checked his cache; today seemed like a perfect time. No one was home. Tyler's sister was busy with her girlfriends at some school meeting, and his mother was at work. He was always glad when she was working because it usually meant that she wasn't drinking; those were the occasions when he was most afraid of her.

He went out to the garage, moved the lawn mower away from the back wall, and saw the faint outline of cracked sheetrock. Almost a year ago, he accidentally banged one of the mower's front wheels against the wall, and it created a small hole in the siding. The top half of the broken piece was still attached by the sheetrock's paper coating, and by pushing against the broken piece, it swung inward, as if on a hinge. It created an opening large enough for him to insert his hand. That's where he had been hiding them.

He reached in and pulled out the two panties he had taken from the clothesline. Fondling them, he hardly felt any stirring, not at all like the time that he saw his sister and the darkness through her panties. He wanted those feelings again, but now, simply seeing or touching the panties didn't seem to be doing it. He needed something more.

He thought his best opportunity for once again having those pleasant sexual sensations would be to "accidently" encounter his sister as she walked around the house in her underwear. When she was home, like after school, he would stay in his room, across the hallway from hers, and watch for her to head toward the bathroom, hoping to get a glimpse of her in her panties. Unfortunately, he was unsuccessful; several times she left her room to shower, but each time she had worn a bathrobe. Maybe, he speculated, she no longer saw him as her little kid brother.

Where else could he observe a girl in her panties? Then it struck him: imagine, he thought, if he could observe the bikini lady in her underpants and maybe even see dark hair underneath. Just the idea of it was stimulating.

He decided to start by checking out her house. He didn't know if any of the three windows facing her backyard were for her bedroom. He surmised that the middle window, smaller than the other two, was probably a bathroom.

At Tyler's first opportunity, from his upstairs hallway window, he used his binoculars to look down over the fence into the windows. Unfortunately, the angle only revealed a small section of each room's floor; it wasn't possible to figure out which one, if any, was her bedroom. The only way he'd know for sure, he thought, would be to peek in each of the windows.

A few weeks later, Tyler was home from school early. He was alone in the house. Outside, the neighborhood seemed deserted; almost everyone sought shelter inside because it was oppressively humid, with temperatures in the high nineties. Thunderstorms were imminent. A perfect afternoon to find out which window opened into her bedroom.

At one corner of the fence, Tyler found some loose boards that could easily be pushed aside. Without much effort, he parted them and casually slipped through the narrow opening. As he neared the house, lightning lit the sky and was quickly followed by thunder. He knew he'd have to move fast.

As Tyler quickly stepped up onto the concrete patio, he noticed a door directly in front of him. It looked like it might lead to the kitchen. More or less automatically, he grabbed the doorknob, and to his amazement, it opened!

CHAPTER 18

Signal Twenty-One R

For the next two hours, our patrol was relatively uneventful—one fender bender with no injuries and minor damage, and a man who fell in a parking lot. He was shaken up but not seriously hurt. He refused an ambulance.

We were slowly cruising the airport roadways, chatting about what I was learning at the academy, when the peacefulness was disrupted: "One-three-one-two, a twenty-one R at 481 Seabrook Avenue, female complainant will be waiting at the door, case 331901."

"One-three-one-two, ten-four."

Off we sped. I was immediately energized.

"Do you know what the radio signal twenty-one R means?" Jose asked.

"I think twenty-one is a burglary, but I forget what the R means."

"R means it's a residential burglary."

"Look, Jerry, we don't know what we're going to run into. There could be a perp or more on the premises, or maybe no one. When we get there, we'll do as we did with the traffic stop. You wait outside the car close to the radio. When I make contact, I'll tell you what to do next."

"Got it."

We traveled a mile or so through residential streets lined with small houses and condo buildings. While not new, most of the buildings seemed well kept; lawns were cut, and most of the residences were landscaped with palm trees and flowering shrubs. Within five minutes, Jose turned onto Seabrook Avenue. The house at 481 turned out to be a gray-colored, stucco, one-story building with a red tile roof and black faux shutters. A concrete driveway led to a one-car garage. All in all, it appeared well cared for.

As Jose stopped at the curb at the corner of the lot, a woman opened the front door and waved to us.

Jose grabbed the radio microphone and said, "One-three-one-two, ten-ninety-seven female at doorway."

"One-three-one-two, do you want me to hold the air?"

"One-three-one-two, negative," Jose replied.

Jose got out of the car and called up to the woman, "Is anyone else in the house?"

"No, it's just me," she called back.

"Jerry," Jose said, "you can tag along. Bring your notepad. As we go through the house, note each room we're in and write down everything she says. I'll be taking notes as well."

We climbed the steps onto a small, concrete stoop. Jose introduced us, and she quickly replied, "I'm *so* glad you're here. My name is Nikki Wilson. Come in."

She appeared to be about forty. Tall, maybe 5' 10." She was wearing green medical scrubs, and hanging from her neck was a plastic name card that read "Ocean County Medical System, N. Wilson, RN." She was tense; the lines around her eyes and mouth were taut, and her hands were trembling.

"All right, ma'am, have you been through the house?" Jose asked. "Are you certain that there is no one in there?"

"Yes, I've been in every room. Whoever it was is gone."

"Okay, let's walk through each room. Tell us if anything is missing or disturbed."

She led the way into the living room. Everything was neat and tidy. Tables were dusted; chairs and lamps seemed to be carefully placed. It looked as though the house was prepped for a real estate showing.

"Nothing missing here," she said.

Next, we went through a small dining room—again nothing missing—and then into the kitchen. As we entered it, Nikki abruptly stopped, as if there was something dangerous ahead.

"There," she said as she pointed to a bare countertop. "That's what I noticed first, that soda can. I don't drink soda. I only keep it for company. I definitely did not leave that can out on the counter."

Jose and I saw what she meant. Standing alone, like a cactus in the desert, was a can of Diet Coke. It appeared to be unopened. "Have you touched it?" asked Jose.

"No, I'm afraid to go near it."

"Okay, let's leave it for now."

We continued the tour through a small guest bedroom and a bathroom, which had a second door that opened to her bedroom. Then we entered the only remaining room, Nikki's bedroom. Everything was tidy; the bed was made, and not a shoe or piece of clothing was lying about. Not like my bedroom.

"Look at that," Nikki said as she pointed to her dresser. It was feminine looking, painted pale blue with some floral designs here and there. As Jose and I followed the direction of her pointing finger, we noticed that the top drawer on the left was half-open. As we neared the dresser, we saw that it was filled with underwear. Unlike the tidiness in the rest of the house, it was a messy jumble of panties and bras; a couple of panties were even dangling over the sides of the drawer.

"That was closed when I left this morning," she said, "and the underwear was neatly organized. Not like that. I can't believe this. Somebody was rummaging in that drawer!"

CHAPTER 19

An Offense

In my mind, the word *burglar* conjures the image of a furtive-looking man wearing a mask, holding a drawn gun, and carrying a big cloth sack. But panties? What is that all about? Is it even a crime?

It led to my recalling, when I was in junior high, giggling locker room conversations about college kids who were more into panty raids than American history.

Jose interrupted my reverie. "Ma'am, do you have a pen or pencil handy?"

"Yes, I do," said Nikki, "right here in my night table."

Jose then asked her to use the pen to poke through the drawer to see if any articles were missing. She looked uncomfortable, perhaps a bit embarrassed sorting through her undies in front of us. When she finished, she said that she could not say for certain if anything was missing—maybe a panty or two.

I don't know what got into me, but I suddenly blurted out, "How did he get in?"

Jose glanced at me with a who-told-you-to-lead-the-investigation frown. "I'll handle it, Jerry," he warned.

"Ma'am, we didn't notice any broken doors or windows. Was anything open when you came into the house?"

"No, nothing was open. I came in from the driveway to my front door, and I needed my key to open it; it was locked. But the kitchen door, the one leading to my backyard, was unlocked. I always lock up the house when I leave, but maybe I missed it this time. I don't know; I'm so upset I can't think straight."

"That's understandable, ma'am. It's an easy thing to overlook. Let's go and look at the door."

The three of us went through the kitchen to the rear door. It opened to a small fenced-in yard. Directly outside of the door was a small brick patio, a lounge, two white-painted Adirondack chairs, and a small, round table.

The door's locking mechanism was a simple door handle / lock combination. No deadbolt. Jose put on plastic gloves, opened the door, and examined the lock but apparently saw nothing broken or out of place.

"Do you have your key handy?" Jose asked.

"It's in my purse. I'll get it."

Jose used Nikki's key to lock and unlock the door; everything seemed to work perfectly.

"I can't believe I left it unlocked," Nikki once again bemoaned.

"Maybe you didn't forget," Jose said. "The burglar could have had a master key or tools to open the door. It's pretty common."

"Oh, no!" she shouted. "That means anybody could get in here, even when I'm home at night!"

I felt sorry for her. I would have been frightened too. Having had no experience with emotional, adult females, I couldn't think of what to do or say to reassure her. But Jose came to the rescue. He suggested that maybe no one tampered with the lock; it was unlocked, and the burglar simply walked in. He also told her about Zachery's, a twenty-four-hour locksmith on Seventeenth Street. He recommended that she install a new lock with a deadbolt.

"Jerry, here's the trunk key. Go out and bring in the camera and an evidence bag."

When I returned, Jose directed me to take a few pictures of each room and several of the soda can, the opened dresser drawer, and the back door with its lock mechanism. Then we returned to the kitchen, and with his gloved hands, Jose picked up and examined the can and then told me to hold open an evidence bag.

I was thinking, *Hey, Mom, I'm at a crime scene; I'm a real investigator!* I never thought that a routine, one-day riding assignment would give me this much real-life police exposure.

Jose explained to Nikki that we were going to be in the area for a few more minutes and that he'd put our patrol car in her driveway. He then wrapped things up by telling her that she'd next hear from a detective. He gave her his card and told her to call if she discovered anything else missing or if she needed help.

When we were back at the car, Jose backed in her driveway and said that we were going to canvas the neighbors and that I should come with him. We visited the houses on either side of Nikki's and two others directly across the street. One was unoccupied and had a "For Sale" sign near the curb. At the other three houses we visited, no one answered our knocks.

We returned to the police car and drove around the block to Palm Meadow Avenue. There were three houses there that had backyards abutting Ms. Wilson's.

At the first house, a short, overweight man answered our knock. When he appeared in the doorway, he was in the midst of buttoning up a long-sleeved work shirt.

"I'm on my way to work. What's happening?"

Jose explained that there was a burglary in the neighborhood and that we were checking to see if he had seen anyone prowling around.

"No, I work a night shift, and I just woke up. I didn't see anything or anybody. I have to hustle now, or I'm going to be late for my job."

Jose asked his name. We learned it was Bruce McPherson, and then Jose said that if he recalled anything suspicious, to please call the police. Jose gave him a card with his name and number.

At the second house, the one directly behind Nikki's, a female teenager (maybe fifteen or sixteen) responded to our knock. She had light brown hair with attractive blonde streaks and was wearing torn jeans and T-shirt. Rap music was blaring somewhere in the house. She seemed startled to see us and quickly stepped back from the doorway.

"Is something wrong?"

"No, ma'am," replied Jose, going through his generic explanation.

"I haven't seen anything," she said. "I only got home from school about an hour ago."

"Have you seen anyone walking in the neighborhood that you don't know or who doesn't live here?"

"No, the only person who seems to be in and out of the neighborhood is a guy who sprays the lawns, you know, for bugs and stuff. Maybe fertilizer."

"Did you see him today?"

"No, but he's around a lot."

"Do you know his name or the company he works for?" asked Jose.

"I wouldn't know his name—he doesn't do our lawn—but he has this green-colored van, and the company name is something like Lawns and Gardens. I just don't remember it."

"What is your name?"

"I'm Sally Clifford."

"Thank you, Sally. Here's my card. If you think of anyone we should check out, please call me."

Nobody was home at the third house abutting Nikki's backyard. I began to see how frustrating police investigations can be.

Once back in the car, I asked Jose, "Now what?"

"We write an IO report."

"What's that?"

"Oops, sorry, Jerry. IO stands for Incident/Offense Report. The call we just responded to was an offense—a burglary with no property loss. We're going to drive to a quiet place in that park on Oak Street and fill it out while everything is fresh in our minds. We'll compare our notes and cull out the most helpful information. At the end of our shift, we'll give it to the sergeant; he'll approve it and then send it to the Detective Bureau, where a detective will be assigned."

It seems like an awfully slow process, but I decided not to say anything.

CHAPTER 20

Horror Scene

To my surprise, I was feeling anxious and uncomfortable, much like you feel when you misplace your car keys. Maybe it stemmed from the lack of closure; we didn't catch the bad guy at Nikki's. *Oh well*, I said to myself, trying to dismiss the uneasiness. *The FBPD are in charge, and they're probably handling it the way they find best.*

It was about seven o'clock, and we had just ordered our dinner at the Beach Diner when Jose's shoulder-mounted radio, on low volume, announced, "One-three-one-two, female who called in an earlier twenty-one R just called in a nine-one-one. Sounds hysterical. Keeps saying she's threatened. I know you're on dinner break; do you want me to assign another unit?"

Jose turned to me and asked, "Do you want to eat or take the call?"

"Let's go," I immediately replied. I couldn't eat knowing Nikki was in trouble.

"One-three-one-two, ten-four to 481 Seabrook."

It wasn't quite dark when we pulled up across the street from of Nikki's house, but every one of her windows was brightly lit. She must have been watching out for us because the front door immediately opened and Nikki appeared in the entrance way, silhouetted against the hall lights.

Jose opened his car door and shouted to Nikki, "Is anyone else there?"

"No," she shouted back. "Please help me!"

She did sound hysterical.

"Jerry, stand by your car door. I'm going to check it out."

"Yes, sir."

I noticed that Jose carried his flashlight in his weak hand and loosened the strap on his holster. He slowly walked across the street toward the stoop. He and Nikki conversed for a few minutes, and then Jose waved, signaling for me to come join him.

When I neared the doorway, I saw that Nikki's hair was wet and stringy, hanging down onto her shoulders; she must have just come out of a shower. She was wearing a white bathrobe. As she gestured with her arms, I could see her nipples move beneath the robe. Obviously, that was all that she had on. My hormones were working just fine; I found it a struggle to focus on her words and not her body.

"He's coming back," she screamed. It appeared that she wanted to bring me up to date on what she had told Jose on the stoop. "I'll show you."

She turned around and quickly led us farther into the house, heading directly toward the bathroom. It was still warm and a bit steamy. Nikki pointed to the large mirror directly over the sink. We looked at the mirror but didn't see anything unusual. Jose and I turned toward each other with puzzled looks.

"Oh, my God," said Nikki. "It was right there," she said, again pointing her finger toward the center of the mirror.

"What was right there?"

"A note. A note. As soon as I got out of the shower, I saw it."

"What do you mean?" Jose inquired. "A note was taped to the mirror?"

"No, no," Nikki responded with impatience and a touch of anger. "It was written on the mirror."

"And now it's disappeared?"

"Yes. It was there when I stepped out of the shower."

"So," said Jose, "is anything different now from how it was when you spotted the sign?"

"Everything's the same. I saw it as soon as I stepped out of the shower."

"Okay," said Jose. "Maybe the room was more steamed up when you got out of the shower. Ma'am, please turn on the shower's hot water faucet, and let's see what happens."

After a few minutes, the bathroom became thick with steam, and then slowly, in the center of the mirror appeared narrow streaks that did not steam up. They formed crudely written block letters that read: "I'LL SEE U."

"What does that mean?" Nikki asked in a panic-stricken voice. "It sounds like he's coming back! He said he's going to see me. Or what? Spy on me?"

"Don't touch anything," Jose quietly said.

Handing me the car keys, Jose ordered, "Jerry, go out and get the camera.

"Ma'am, what is your phone number?"

When I returned with the camera, Jose was on the radio. "HQ, one-three-one-two, I need a crime scene unit to 481 Seabrook Avenue. The phone here is 904-111-3943."

"I can't believe this is happening," Nikki wailed. "It's a nightmare!"

Nikki seemed completely distraught. I had never seen anyone look as distressed, except maybe my mother when her younger sister, Margie, died suddenly. Everything about Nikki seemed rigid, taut—her arms, her legs, her face. Her face was ashen, her eyes open wide. They looked dark and vacuous. Trembling fingers absentmindedly kept touching her lips, covering her mouth. Thinking that she might collapse, I quickly asked, "Can I get you a chair?"

I thought that Jose might not like my intervention, but he made no sign of disapproval.

"No, I'm all right," Nikki replied, "but can we sit down in the living room?"

As the three of us walked away from the bathroom, I realized that I had just learned something about crime that I had never appreciated—that a minor crime can have major consequences. In this case, a simple break-in resulted in a life-changing experience. While the burglary was the official crime, the greater, unrecorded and hidden crime was the victim's psychological damage.

If I ever had doubts about pursuing a career in law enforcement, this patrol call eliminated those reservations. I wanted to be in the fight to prevent more Nikki-like experiences.

CHAPTER 21

Now What?

As we sat in the living room, Nikki resumed her plaintive cries, "What am I going to do? What am I going to do?"

I wasn't sure what to say, but Jose immediately took charge. In a quiet, relaxed tone, he said, "There's lots to do, ma'am. We're going to work this out; you'll be safe. As a start, why don't you get dressed, and then we'll talk about some positive things we can do."

"Okay, I'll just be a few minutes."

"Take your time. We'll be here. Please don't touch anything in the bathroom."

Under Jose's direction, I took six photos of the message on the bathroom mirror, and then he and I returned to the living room. He asked me to use my phone and research some websites for home security and electricians.

Nikki reappeared. She looked somewhat better than when she left us; her tenseness seemed to be abated; her eyes were more relaxed, and her hands had stopped trembling. She wore faded jeans and a loose T-shirt stenciled, "Go Jaguars." Her hair was pulled back into a ponytail, which, I thought, made her look younger.

"I'm so scared. What can we do?"

"Ma'am, is it all right for us to call you Nikki?"

"Of course," she quickly responded.

"Nikki, as we've said, we're not going to leave you alone. But you need support, someone you know and trust. Do you have a friend or relative you can call that will come over to be with you?"

"My best friend is Dora. She's a nurse at the hospital, but I hate to trouble her."

"Would it be easier if I made the call?" Jose asked. "I'm happy to do it."

"No, no. That's all right. I'll call her. She should be home by now."

Nikki dialed the number, but Dora didn't pick up. Her voice mail spewed the standard request about leaving a message, but Nikki was so rattled that she just hung up. She was sobbing again.

"Who else do you trust?"

"Well, of course, my sister, Penny, Penelope. But she lives over in Flagler Beach. It would take her a half hour or more to get here."

"We're sticking around. Let's not worry about the time. Give her a ring."

Nikki made the call and briefly explained the situation, and her sister said that she would be there within an hour. With that news, I already felt better. I wondered how much it relieved Nikki.

"Nikki, while we're waiting for Penelope, let's talk about ways to help make your home more protected. Did you call the locksmith yet?

"Yes, I phoned Zachery's right after you left. He said he'd be here about seven. Oh my, it's way past seven already."

With that comment, the doorbell rang.

"I'll get it," said Jose.

The caller was Jonathan Zachery himself. Apparently, he and Jose knew each other, and they warmly chatted while walking into the living room. Jose introduced Jonathon to Nikki and me, and then all of us went to the back door to discuss options for making it more secure. Nikki's tears ceased.

We stood around for a while, watching the locksmith install an entirely new door knob/lock fixture—one that he claimed was almost impossible to pick. Then we returned to the living room and began a discussion about other security measures. Jose explained how an alarm system and motion-sensitive floodlights could give her greater peace of mind.

We had just started searching for alarm systems when the doorbell once again rang. It was Penelope. I presumed that she sped most of the way.

Penelope quickly brushed past Jose and me and ran toward Nikki, her arms openly extended for an embrace. The two women hugged each other, both talking at the same time and also crying. Quite a scene. But even though tears were being shed, the atmosphere was becoming less tense; Nikki even seemed energized as she tried to describe to Penelope all that had transpired since she had come home from work. I took my cue from Jose and stood quietly aside while they focused on each other.

At that point, Mr. Zachary came into the living room. He told Nikki that he had finished the installation and wanted to give her the keys and show her how the new lock worked. And so, off they went, the locksmith leading the way, and Nikki and Penelope trailing along, still animatedly talking to each other.

About then, we heard on Jose's shoulder radio a female voice report, "CSI two, ten-ninety-seven at 481 Seabrook."

"That's our crime scene unit," said Jose. "I'll let her in."

The CSI officer, a woman, looked to be about thirty—young, I thought, to be a crime scene expert. In any case, she introduced herself as Alexandria Constantine and quickly said that everyone calls her "Alex." She came across as serious and businesslike—hardly any smiles and little spontaneity. I guessed that she was five feet or less, compact looking. Short black hair framed a round, tanned face. She wore a polo shirt and slacks almost the same color blue as my trainee uniform.

It was getting to be a crowded place. "It's like Grand Central," I quietly uttered—a phrase my father often used when there was commotion in our house.

CHAPTER 22

Wrapping Up

Alex asked Jose to bring her up to date on everything that had happened and to show him the crime scenes. Jose said, "Jerry, wait here in the living room for Nikki and Penelope. It will help if we can keep them busy, so I want you to continue with them, maybe having them jot down two or three companies they could call."

It was a bummer not being invited to go on the walk-through with Alex, but I had an assignment, and that diminished my disappointment. I wondered how many first-time-riding trainees were ever required to keep a victim busy.

In a short while, Nikki and Penelope returned and said goodbye to the locksmith, and there I was, alone with the two women. Both of them were old enough to be my mother! I felt incredibly uncomfortable and uncertain about how to proceed, so I just blurted out, "Do you want to do as Officer Hernandez suggested and try to find some good alarm companies and electricians?"

"That sounds like a good idea," said Penelope, coming to my rescue. "What to do you think, Nikki?"

"Okay," she answered softly.

Here I was, a nineteen-year-old kid, trying to direct these women. I had the temerity to say, "We'll need to jot down the companies and their telephone numbers."

To my surprise, Nikki volunteered. She said, "I'll get a notepad and pen, but they're in the kitchen. Can I go in there?"

"I'm not sure," I said. "The CSI person is probably in the kitchen or maybe in your bedroom. Just ask Officer Hernandez; he'll know what to do."

I was surprised I said that with so much authority. *Hey,* I thought, *I'm becoming a cop!*

The atmosphere, which earlier was laden with anxiety, had changed. Nikki's voice now seemed almost free of tension; she was actually speaking in a relaxed manner, as though she were chatting with friends. And, in an animated discussion, Penelope and Nikki selected two alarm companies and two electricians. Nikki agreed to call them in the morning.

"Nikki, what are your plans for tonight?" asked Jose. "Will you stay here, go to a motel, or what?"

"Penny and I have been talking about that. We'll stay here, and she'll also be here tomorrow to help me interview the alarm people and electricians."

Jose's interaction with Nikki was a powerful lesson for me. His efforts—the offering of constructive suggestions for beefing up security and his promise not to leave her

90

alone—had to be comforting to Nikki. I hadn't visualized cops playing that kind of supportive role.

"That sounds good," Jose said. "Jerry and I have other calls to attend to, so we'll be leaving now. You have my card with the case number; don't hesitate to call if you discover anything new or you feel threatened.

"By the way, Alex will be here for a while, and she'll want to review with you all that took place tonight. Are you up for it?"

"I think I can manage it." She continued on, fumbling for the right words, "I can't thank you enough for helping me through this ordeal. I was a basket case, and you were there for me. And, Jerry, you'll make a fine policeman."

I felt my face redden. I couldn't believe I was blushing at the compliment.

It was well after nine o'clock when we closed the front door and began walking toward the patrol car. I was elated. What a ride-along. I thought we had really done something good that night. I saw Jose as a great role model.

"Well, Jerry, we're back in service, and we still need to write the report about this crime. Are you starving? We could go to a drive-through and pick up something, or if it will hold you, I've got an extra granola bar here you can have."

I was so excited about the day's events that, even though I was hungry, eating didn't seem that important. I also sensed that Jose felt pressured to get the report completed before our shift ended. "Thanks, Jose. Let's get to work."

HQ was quiet. I didn't see anyone, so I assumed that the other recruits had long since left. It was nearing eleven o'clock when I finally got to my car.

Amazingly, despite the long day, I wasn't feeling tired. I began reminiscing about my adventure—how Jose had me carry the shotguns, learning to use them, getting comfortable with the radio, the traffic stop, the calls to 481 Seabrook, Nikki, and being directly involved in the investigation.

I wondered how the other trainees fared, and my mind lingered on Bridge. I visualized what she looked like and how pretty she was. I wished she was there right then.

CHAPTER 23

Monday

Monday morning. The alarm jolted me awake amid the sound of rain furiously hitting my bedroom window. Raising the shade, I peeked out and was greeted by a gray sky filled with dark, almost black clouds. The rain seemed unrelenting.

But the gloomy scene didn't deter me in the least. I was invigorated and eager to get to the academy to compare notes with my classmates about their riding assignments.

My enthusiasm, however, was quickly tempered as I drove along a busy Center Street. An accident, somewhere ahead, had the traffic at a standstill. There were no nearby side streets; I was stuck.

When I finally arrived at the academy, I thought it still might be possible to make class on time. As I dashed toward the classroom building, my jacket shed the rain, but my unprotected pants were soaked before I got to the entrance door. Glancing at my watch, I discovered that I was only one minute late. But, unfortunately, I arrived at my desk just as Sergeant Gagnon was beginning a tirade about memorizing the radio codes. *Damnit*, I thought, *I'm fucked.*

"Hey, recruit," he shouted as he pointed at me, "what are you stupid or something, trying to sneak in here late?"

It sounded as though he was setting me up, hoping I would mention some lame excuses that he could tear apart. But I was learning how to play the game. Even more important, after my riding assignment, I felt that I was already a cop, badge or no badge. I was learning to anticipate, and it gave me balls.

"Yes, sir!" I shouted loud and clear.

He blinked—for a split second, revealing his surprise at my admittance. "And why are you stupid, Krone?"

"Sir, I wasn't smart enough to allow time for a major accident on my drive to the academy this morning."

"You should always plan for the worse scenario," he lectured. "Remember that. And don't ever try to outfox me, Krone; you'll lose." But he had already lost, and he knew it.

The sergeant continued, "I'm going to check on this morning's accident reports, and if I find that you're lying to me, you're finished here. Do you hear me?"

"Yes, sir," I replied.

"Now get down on the floor and show the class how you do twenty push-ups."

"Yes, sir."

I realized that this incident could be a problem for the remainder of my academy stay; it all depended upon the sergeant's objectivity. He might rate me as a wiseass. Or he could evaluate me as someone who was not easily bullied. I'd have to wait to see how it fell out. It was not the beginning I wanted on my first day back.

CHAPTER 24

Bridge

When lunch break was announced, I glanced over my shoulder to try to spot Tony, Rico, and Bridge. Guess who was looking right at me? I felt thrilled and wondered if she felt the same.

I didn't have to ask her to lunch; it just happened. As luck would have it, Tony and Rico were caught up with some other guys and didn't appear to be seeking us out. So, there we were, Bridge and I.

At the table, conversation seemed effortless.

She was grinning. Then, excitedly, she queried, "So, how did it go?"

"Great," I said, "but you tell me first."

"You're sure?"

"Yes, please."

"Well, don't mind if I do. It was interesting but sort of dull," she volunteered. "Walt, my FTO—he's an older dude. He's got three years left before retirement, and I think he's a bit lacking in the inspiration department. He told me, 'If it doesn't come over the radio, I don't get involved.' So, that gives you an idea of how the day went."

"Did he teach you how to use the shotguns and the radio?"

"I carried two shotguns to the car, but he just stowed them and didn't show me anything about firing them. I did learn, though, how to use the radio and to listen for our call sign.

"The only radio call we responded to was for a stolen bike. We interviewed the bike's owner, a young girl, Pauline, and her mother. We learned that the theft happened fifteen minutes earlier (she had parked it outside of Dairy Queen). So, Walt had me take notes as he asked for a description of the bike and serial number. We canvassed—I think that's the word he used. Anyway, we walked to the neighboring stores and asked about the bike, but no one claimed to have seen it.

"After Walt radioed dispatch a BOLO for a 'girl's bright red Schwinn with a blue and white handlebar basket,' we cruised the neighborhood searching for it. And guess what? I spotted the bike!"

"Well, that only sounds a *little* boring," I brilliantly commented. "But you saved the day!"

"I know," she said, rolling her eyes with a grin. "Quite the hero."

I had never been this close to Bridge's face. Her eyes were sparkling. They were soft and light blue, what I think of as baby blue.

"It was an exciting moment. The bike was hidden in some bushes bordering the Walmart parking lot."

When they returned the bike, Bridge described how the joy of getting her bike back brought Pauline to tears. It had been a Christmas present. Bridge said the whole episode made her feel good about deciding to be a cop.

She said that the remainder of her tour was uneventful. Walt did a traffic stop—a missing license plate. But that turned out to be routine because the driver had the plate on the passenger seat and was on his way to the hardware store to buy some screws.

"Most of the time, we drove around town. You're looking at Fortuna's newest expert on every city border, dead end, and street number," she sarcastically proclaimed. "But he did show me how to search the airport parking lots for stolen cars," she said. "And took me to Margo's, his favorite place for dinner." She added that Walt told her it was traditional for recruits to pick up the tab on their first riding assignment, which she did.

"And now, what about you?" Bridge asked.

CHAPTER 25

Jerry

"Bridge, I had an incredible riding assignment. Like you, we had a traffic stop, but the highlight of my ride was a twenty-one R call. I remembered that twenty-one meant burglary, but Jose, my FTO, had to tell me that the R stood for residence."

"Oh," Bridge interrupted, "I remember hearing that call, but I didn't know, of course, that it was your car that responded. And wasn't there a second call to the same place?"

"Yes, we were one-three-one-two, and that was us handling both."

I explained how the calls unfolded and all about Nikki and the threatening sign that mysteriously appeared on the mirror. Bridge became caught up in my excitement. Her eyes widened as she leaned in closer so as to not miss a word.

"Nikki must have been horrified; it makes me shiver just thinking about it," said Bridge, hugging herself.

I described the angst on Nikki's face and how her fears gradually diminished when Jose assured her that we wouldn't leave her alone and that there were steps she could take to make her house more secure.

"Still," said Bridge, worrying, "she must be petrified knowing he said that he'd 'see her.' I know I would. Do you think they'll catch the guy?"

"I don't know. They're assigning a detective to the case, and even before we left the scene, the CS investigator was dusting for fingerprints and looking for DNA samples. I just hope they get him. On my next riding assignment, that's the first thing I'm going to ask about."

"Well, for your first riding assignment, you had some cool police experiences; I bet you can't wait to get back out again."

"You're right," I said. "I feel like a cop already."

All at once, the cafeteria was quiet, and when I looked up, I saw that almost everyone had left. Clearly, the lunch hour was over. It surprised me because it seemed as if we had been chatting for only a few minutes. Bridge made it easy for me to express my thoughts; she was a good listener. It was also very nice being able to talk without the fear of being judged.

As Bridge and I stood to leave the table, she put her hand on top of mine and said, "Jerry, your riding assignment was really cool. I can't wait to find out what the police did and how Nikki is doing. Thanks for sharing it with me."

As we walked back to the classroom, I continued to feel the warm glow that occurred when Bridge's hand rested on mine. For her, perhaps it was merely a casual touch, a meaningless gesture, but for me, it was a special moment.

CHAPTER 26

Bright Lights in the Daily Grind

Even though two months remained until my next riding assignment—one that would last an entire week—my time at the academy seemed to whiz by. Eight hours each day were fully occupied with lectures and demonstrations on an incredible range of topics like crime scene investigation, interview techniques, first aid, traffic crash investigation, Florida laws and statutes, and constitutional law. We actually received college credit for all of them. I was pleased to discover classes weren't simply about writing traffic tickets.

Every course involved lots of tests. Fortunately, I scored well on most of them. It helped that I was a fast reader, but also, unlike high school, I was now more conscientious about studying. At the end of our first month, I was one of only three recruits that scored 100 percent on a radio codes test. My chest swelled when sergeant Gagnon actually praised me with a "well done" comment.

Classroom work was interrupted daily with physical conditioning: push-ups, laps, and running that damn obstacle course. As much as most of us hated the strenuous demands, it was noticeable how much less we were panting when we returned to the classroom. I was stronger and in better condition than I had ever been.

The academic classes were also intermingled with some interesting field trips. One day, we went to court and watched a cop take the stand and the oath and then answer the prosecutor's questions. Then we looked on in dismay and alarm as the defense attorney tried to tear his testimony apart. Fortunately, the officer kept his cool and objectivity, despite the lawyer's attempt to twist the cop's testimony.

On the next day, when we returned to the academy, we had a class given by the state's attorney on how to testify. All those who visited the courtroom with me were, as you can imagine, especially attentive.

Another trip was to the morgue to observe an autopsy. The body was that of a black male who had been stabbed. As the autopsy proceeded, I didn't throw up but came close. The odors were terrible. When the coroner began using a circular saw to cut open the victim's skull, I had to step outside to the hallway. I don't think I'd ever make it as a surgeon.

Two other out-of-the-classroom ventures were, for me, the most fun; they involved guns and cars.

CHAPTER 27

Guns

There was a buzz in the air—unspoken and subtle. It was range week. We were going to be issued our guns and commence a week of shooting.

The excitement built slowly. It began with a lecture detailing the county's use-of-force policy, followed by another presentation and two films about gun safety. Gagnon then told us, "Memorize your gun's serial number—you'll be tested on it—and never, never fire it when not on the range. If you do, and we find out, you're done. When you get home with your gun, don't show it off; lock it in a secure place and keep it there until it's time to leave for the range.

"Before you report to the range, buy yourself a gun-cleaning kit. Your squad leader has a list of stores that sell them. And be damn sure to bring it with you in the morning."

I struggled to keep focused on the lecture; I couldn't wait to be handed my gun.

Then came the moment. It was my turn to report to the desk in front of the room. I was presented a 9 mm Glock automatic and three empty magazines. It was a special moment, like a rite of passage. For some reason, I felt humble.

After lunch, the entire class left for the shooting range. It wasn't on campus but in the Western District, located in a wooded, undeveloped section of town, west of I-95. I was surprised at its size. The range looked to be over an acre, enclosed by a ten-foot, wire mesh fence.

As I exited my car, the first thing that caught my attention was an open-sided wooden tower, about fifteen feet high. It was unpainted, roofed, and on its eaves, facing the range, were mounted two large loudspeakers. It reminded me of a guard tower at some prison.

Inside the fence gate were twenty-five firing lanes, each with a human-sized target at the far end. Directly behind all the targets, serving as a backstop, was a high mound of dirt and sand. If you missed your target, your bullet would harmlessly bury in the berm.

Off to the right side of the lanes was a square, wooden building that, I soon learned, was a classroom. A smaller structure next to it was the toilet facility.

We were all directed to enter the classroom where instructors, once again, reviewed our department's use-of-force policy. We were then taught how our Glock pistols operated and how to field strip, clean, and reassemble them.

Everyone was provided with an oversized, white T-shirt with a large stenciled number on the back. Mine was eleven. Three lanes down from me at fourteen was Bridge, and next to her, assigned fifteen, was Charlie, our class clown, a fun guy.

Then, off to the range. We were placed in numerical order according to our shooting experience—the six or so gun-savvy recruits (primarily ex-military), were placed at the left end of the line; the majority of us novice shooters were spread out toward the right.

Standing behind us were seven or eight instructors (about one for every three recruits), but at the military end, only a single instructor was assigned to the half dozen or so experienced shooters.

From an officer in the tower, instructions boomed across the entire area.

"Attention, everyone. Here at the range, we're going to take things slow and easy. We will guide you each step of the way to becoming qualified. Never, ever take any action with your gun or make any movement with it, unless so instructed. Failure to comply will result in immediate dismissal. I'm going to say it again. Failure to comply with our instructions in handling your gun will result in immediate dismissal. There are no exceptions to this rule. Do you understand?"

"Yes, sir."

"Let's hear it. Do you understand?"

All of us recruits loudly responded in unison, "Yes, sir!"

"Safety is our number one concern here. We will proceed only as fast as our slowest person. If you have a question, ask it. There are no stupid questions. If you are at all uncertain about your instructor's direction, raise your hand, ask about it. Is that clear?"

The "Yes, sir" was resounding.

I couldn't believe what I was hearing. It was in such contrast to the put-downs and demands we heard almost every day in the classroom, such as "Right now," "That's a dumb question," and "Get with it, kid."

The drills began with our unloaded Glocks. It went like this: secure gun in holster, unsnap strap, draw gun, aim, pull trigger, return to holster. Everyone in the entire row did the drill at the same time. That drill was repeated over and over, maybe thirty times. After a while, I found myself returning my gun to the holster without even having to look—finally I understood muscle memory. I also began to appreciate the value of those push-ups we'd been forced to do.

For the next two hours, we progressed from pulling the trigger with no bullets in the gun to racking the slide back and injecting one bullet in the chamber and firing it, to eventually firing the entire seventeen-cartridge magazine. With each new drill, we gradually moved, as a group, farther from the targets—first one yard, then three, then seven, and finally fifteen yards.

My arms and shoulders ached. My forearms were quivering. I wondered how much longer I was going to be able to extend my arms out in front of me and steadily hold that two-pound gun—and this was just the first day!

Four o'clock finally arrived. As all of us fired our final volley, an officer announced from the tower speakers, "We are finished for the day. Remove the magazine from your gun. Be certain your gun is empty. Draw back the slide and visually inspect the chamber. Even if it looks empty, insert your finger in the chamber to be certain it is clear. Do it now and then place your gun in your holster and leave it there.

"Now it's brass time. We pick up all the empty cartridges. You will not leave any brass on the range! Just to make it clear: one brass left on the range means one push-up. Two brass, two push-ups. Get it?"

"Yes, sir."

"I can't hear you!"

The "Yes, sir!" was loud.

"Tomorrow morning, at 8:00 a.m., report here at the range. Meanwhile, keep your gun unloaded. Clean it tonight. Tomorrow there will be an inspection, and it will be a bitch!"

CHAPTER 28

A New Dimension

As I left the range and walked to the parking lot, Bridge and I spotted each other. I waved, she waved, and we began moving closer. As we met, we started talking about our firing range experiences, but then I interrupted. "Bridge, there's so much to talk about. How about meeting later at Anthony's so we can relax and share stories over pizza?"

We agreed to meet at seven.

During the past two months, we had hardly been together alone. While we often met for lunch, other recruits were usually present, especially Tony and Rico. Also, we were both still wrapped up in our high school relationships. She had a boyfriend, and I was still dating Janet. But whenever we got to eat lunch by ourselves, we enjoyed being together. Conversation came easily as we spoke about our families and high school experiences.

I sensed that tonight was going to be different from our luncheon get-togethers. I didn't know why, except that maybe it had to do with the dead seriousness of the range experience. Firing the gun changed me some. It was another move away from civilian life; I was clearly taking a path different from my high school buddies, most of whom were off to college. I felt as though I had taken another step toward being more a man and less a kid.

CHAPTER 29

Pizza for Two

When I arrived at Anthony's, I had to drive twice around their parking lot before finding a space. Opening the restaurant's door, I was struck with a barrage of delicious aromas—fresh-baked pizza dough, melting cheese, and cooked sausage—along with the din of a noisy twenties crowd. The place was packed; I wondered if I'd be able to find a place for us to sit.

As I scanned the room, over to the left at a corner table, I glimpsed Bridge. She looked smashing. Her shoulder-length black hair glistened, and combined with a black sleeveless blouse, she had a casual yet sophisticated look.

"Hi, Bridge. You must have gotten here hours ago. Thanks for getting the table."

"Jerry, you're late. Drop and give me twenty," she joked. "No, believe it or not, I've only been here for fifteen minutes. A couple was leaving as I walked in, so I grabbed this table. Lucky us!"

As I looked across the table at Bridge, I thought it was a bit of a miracle that a girl this beautiful had agreed to meet with me. I also noted the envious looks on some guys at nearby tables.

We had only spoken a few words, but already it seemed that we were happy to be together. We even agreed quickly on the pizza we wanted—mushroom, sausage, and green pepper, no onions.

"So, what did you think about the range?" I asked.

"It was terrible," she groaned. "Erica was on my left and Charlie on my right, and they didn't seem to have much trouble at all. My shots were all over the place. It was really embarrassing."

"I'm so sorry."

"You know, I've never held a gun in my life. We don't have guns in our house, so everything about them is new. I hate to admit this, but I was scared to pull the trigger."

I tried to be consoling, but all I could come up with was, "I think that's pretty normal for the first time out."

"Well, maybe at the beginning," she said, "but after several hours of drill, you'd think I'd get over it."

"Yeah, I think experience helps. I used to shoot a rifle at my grandparents' farm, so firing wasn't a problem for me. Did your instructor offer any suggestions?"

"He didn't seem particularly concerned about my performance; the only advice he offered me was to 'slow down.' I'm not really sure what that meant I should do."

"When we get to the range tomorrow, let's see if we can stand next to each other. Maybe I'll see something that would be helpful."

"Good. Yeah, let's do that."

We went to talk about how we decided to become cops, and before we knew it, another hour had passed. It got to be near eleven, and we both sensed that it was time to leave.

Bridge offered to split the tab. "Hey, I asked you to meet here," I said. "It's my treat."

She smiled. "Thanks. Such a gentleman."

I walked with Bridge until she found her car (a Volkswagen Beetle). We stood next to each other as she unlocked her door. It was an awkward moment, but she broke the tension, saying, "Jerry, it was a fun night. I had a great time."

As she said that, we were standing face-to-face, and I believe we both sensed that the moment called for something more than the words "good night." We moved closer, and our lips met—a kiss like putting an exclamation point after "Thank you. It was a lovely evening."

Bridge stepped back, opened her car door, and said, "Jerry, I'll see you in the morning."

"Yep," I said, and I broke into a big smile, resisting the urge to jump into the air and dance back to my car.

CHAPTER 30

A Shock

The next morning, at the range, Bridge and I had no difficulty lining up adjacent to each other. We stayed near the right end of the line, and no one seemed to care about which firing lanes we occupied.

Once again, we started the day firing at the one-yard target, and, upon commands from the tower, we drew our guns, rapidly fired two rounds, and then returned our guns to our holsters. The drill was repeated three times, and Bridge had no problem hitting the target.

But when we advanced to the seven-yard distance, I heard Bridge shout, "Oh, shit!" Apparently, she missed the target entirely, much less the center mass.

As we repeated the "draw, fire, holster up" routine, I completed my firing ahead of Bridge and turned to watch her finish the drill. I'm no expert, but it seemed to me that when she pulled the trigger, she jerked her hand downward.

I remembered having a similar problem when learning to shoot my grandfather's 22. He repeatedly told me, "Squeeze; don't pull the trigger. Squeeze it like you're feeling a tomato, testing to see if it's ripe."

At the next break, I shared that story with Bridge and suggested, "Maybe that's what your instructor meant when he said to slow down'"

"But we're supposed to get the shots off quickly," she said.

"Yes, we are, but I think that hitting the target is far more important, at least for now. I bet that your speed will gradually come."

We had been back to the shooting drills for about fifteen minutes when I heard Bridge call, "Jerry, I'm squeezing the tomato; it's working!"

Bridge was aglow. I felt so proud of her. But about midafternoon, our enthusiasm quickly dampened. We had just finished the fifteen-yard drill when the tower loudspeakers boomed, "Recruit number fifteen, holster your gun. Right now. You were told to secure it in your holster. Leave your firing lane and report to Sergeant Valdez. He is standing right behind you."

"Oh, my God," I quietly uttered. "That's Charlie."

Intense silence overtook the range. Everyone appeared stunned by the arbitrary and harsh words emanating from the speakers. I liked Charlie and feared for the consequences of his actions. Bridge and I could see his arms pleadingly extended. While he was too far away for us to hear his conversation with Sergeant Valdez, I did catch a loudly spoken, "But it wasn't even loaded."

Despite Charlie's protests, both the tower instructor and the sergeant prevailed, and Charlie turned over his weapon and belt. Slowly, head down, he walked through the gate to the parking lot.

When Charlie's car left, the officer in the tower explained, "Number fifteen was charged with a safety violation. When all guns were to be holstered, recruit number nine was drawing and holstering. We warned all of you that instructor directions must be immediately obeyed, no excuses. He was dismissed. If he wants to rejoin the force, he may reapply in a year. Now let's all get back to work."

To say that the announcement was sobering is an incredible understatement. Total silence prevailed. No one wanted to resume shooting; gloom hovered over the entire range. Most of us were feeling sad and, at the same time, angry at the instructors; almost everyone in the class liked Charlie, and it was painful to watch him walking away in disgrace. I felt sorry for him. And yet the incident brought home to me a vivid awareness that being a cop is different, that you have to live by different standards—greater discipline and higher expectations. A month or so ago, I would have rigorously defended Charlie.

CHAPTER 31

Declarations

On Wednesday, after completing the day's second round of shooting, one of the instructors examined my targets and said, "Krone, you've qualified."

I wanted to jump and yell, "Hey, that's great!" but I kept my cool and quietly said, "Great. Thank you." It felt good to have conquered another must-pass hurdle.

My success, however, didn't mean I was finished on the range. The remainder of the week, I participated in all the drills, the same as everyone else.

Bridge qualified on Thursday afternoon, and we decided to celebrate both qualifications by having dinner on Friday night because we both had dates on Saturday with other "friends".

We met at the Salt Life. After ordering and chatting about what happened to Charlie, our shooting experiences, and what we were going to do over the weekend, there was a lull in the conversation. I think both of us sensed that we were waiting, treading water, so to speak, trying to decide if we should be talking about us rather than the world around us. I was uncertain that the timing was right, leery about opening a topic that perhaps Bridge wasn't ready for. But the silence got to me. I took the plunge.

"Bridge, do you want to talk about us?"

"Sure, good idea. Do you want to start?"

"No, but I will. I'm not sure where to begin, but I think of us as more than just friendly classmates. We seem to enjoy being together. I think we really like each other … and, well, you're special to me. There, I've said it."

"You know what? I feel the very same way."

"Really?"

You can imagine how the discussion went on from there: big smiles, words tinged with excitement, growing feelings of closeness, and the clasping of hands. We felt like we'd scratched a lottery ticket and won a thousand dollars!

We talked about wanting to see each other more. But, gradually, the realities of our situation became apparent. Competing for our time were our old high school friends (including romantic attachments) and family relationships, along with academy homework. We agreed that, despite all the pulls and tugs on our time, we would try to see each other at least once every weekend. We also struggled with what to do about our respective current girl and boy friends, and agreed that it would be too hurtful to just drop them. We thought that we could slowly ease our way out of these relationships. It didn't exactly work out that way, but that's another story.

It was quite an evening. No, it was a spectacular evening.

There was more than one kiss in the parking lot.

CHAPTER 32

Cars

A week after we returned from the firing range, our class was introduced to a new subject: "County Chase Policy." This course turned out to be preparation for the next two days at the academy's driving range.

I'd been driving a car since I was sixteen and believed I could handle one as well as anybody. Initially, I didn't see any value in spending time at the driving range, but it didn't take long to find out how wrong I was.

The range, located on campus, was a short distance from our classroom building. It was a paved, acre-sized lot with low bleachers on two of its sides. Orange and white traffic cones were lined up to create car-width roads that swirled around the range.

Parked on the range were four specially equipped police cars, each with a brake pedal on the passenger side. At one end of the range was an elevated metal scoreboard, listing each recruit's name along with another column titled "Cones Hit."

"Krone, come with me," said the instructor. "I hear from some of your buddies that ya think you're a hotshot driver."

In a strong New York City accent, he continued, "Let's see how ya do. I'm gonna show ya how you hafta drive ta qualify."

With that, he had me drive, clockwise, once around a narrow, oval-shaped road that ran around the perimeter of the lot. Cones, closely spaced, designated the edges of the road; on the right edge, the roadway was interrupted from time to time by car-length openings that led to a second lane.

"Okay, Krone, get up ta thirty and drive around the oval without hitting any cones."

A cinch, I thought. And it was. I nicked one cone, and it barely tumbled over. Once back at the starting point, he instructed me to go around once again, this time without striking a cone. I was successful and felt my confidence return.

"Now," my instructor said, "go around again, this time at fifty miles per hour." As I started, he turned on the siren and lights. Adrenaline started flowing, and on the first sharp turn, I oversteered, knocking down several cones before I got the car straightened out. It happened again on the next turn. It took two reruns before I got the hang of it.

For the third round, he told me to proceed at forty miles per hour and to weave in and out of my lane by steering through ramp-like openings as they appeared, one after the other.

I'm embarrassed to tell you how many cones I knocked over, but that was nothing to what came next. When I finished the lane-changing exercise, the instructor had me stop the car and repeat the drill, this time by driving backward. Disaster.

When the practice exercise was completed and I walked toward the bleachers where my squad and other classmates were sitting and watching (awaiting their turn to drive), the catcalls began: "Hey, Jerry, do you really have a driver's license?" "Maybe you should try the mounted police." "Did you leave your glasses at home?"

The instructor, who was walking by, looked at the class and said, "Don't laugh too hard. Your turn is coming."

I was further humiliated when I looked up at the scoreboard and saw next to KRONE, in the "Cones Hit" column, a big "22." It was bad but definitely not the worst; some scores were in thirties and forties.

I soon learned that, as in PGA golf tournaments, there is a cut-off score. On any particular drill, if your best score is higher than ten, you must keep trying until you qualify (hit no cones). If you don't qualify, you have to take remedial classes with the next class. If you fail to qualify then, you're gone.

Once everyone in our squad had driven with the instructor, we were allowed several hours to practice on our own. When it was your turn to practice-drive, some of your squad piled into the car. Then the fun began. Smartass remarks about the driver's abilities kept the backseat crowd laughing, but the teasing also relieved a lot of tension. Once in a while, a constructive suggestion—especially when driving backward—helped us avoid cones.

As the day progressed, new drills were introduced: the pit maneuver (a controlled crash to force a car off the road), controlling skids, and managing slippery, wet pavements. These drills were difficult and usually required several runs with the instructor in the passenger seat.

The good news is that by the end of the two days, all our squad qualified. I learned, though, that two recruits didn't make the cut and had to sign up for remedial work; one of them decided to quit the academy. From our initial twenty-nine recruits, we were now down to twenty-six.

CHAPTER 33

Second Riding Assignment

On Friday of the week that we returned from the driving range came the announcement I had been waiting for: "Next week, starting on Sunday, you will be going out on your weeklong riding assignment. Here are the times and dates. You may be assigned to either the Western Station or to the HQ station."

I was assigned the graveyard shift—2200 to 0600 hours—at HQ, the Eastern Station. I had heard that nights could be incredibly boring but were often interrupted by moments of sheer terror. I wondered what new crime scenes I might encounter and what I might learn about Nikki's case.

When I arrived at HQ for roll call, I felt a lot more comfortable than during my first visit. This time, the only unknown was the kind of FTO I would be assigned. That was quickly resolved.

As the roll call meeting was nearing its end, the sergeant began announcing the riding assignment pairings. The first name mentioned was mine. "Molinara, your trainee is Jerry Krone."

With that pronouncement, a cop emerged from the group of officers and began walking toward the back of the room where we recruits were standing. He appeared to be in his fifties, tall (maybe six two), a little overweight but not fatty looking, black hair with a few gray streaks, and a grouchy face distinguished by a long white scar running down his left cheek. My eyes were drawn to it. I imagined that there was quite an interesting story attached to how it got there.

He called out, "Where's Krone?"

"Here, sir."

"Okay, grab your gear and the shotguns and let's get going. How old are you, kid?"

"Nineteen."

"Well then, you don't know shit. I've been on the job for twenty-eight years—I've seen it all. You can learn from me, but I'm telling you, right up front, I'm not a teacher; I'm not going to mollycoddle you. If you don't learn anything, I don't give a damn. It's your loss. But when we get out there, you might learn something by doing whatever I tell you.

"By the way, my name is Francis Molinara, but I go by Frank. You call me Francis and I'll shut your mouth with my fist. Capito?"

It was clear that Frank was no Jose and that this riding assignment was going to challenge my patience. I was bristling already, and we had only been together for a few minutes.

As we continued to walk toward the car, Frank peppered me with questions: "Did you qualify on at the range? Driving? Do you know how to use the radio? Do you know the radio codes?"

I was able to respond yes to his questions, but I wasn't even certain that that was a plus; maybe it only raised his expectations of me. I was annoyed with myself for feeling intimidated.

"Jerry, tonight your job is to watch me. I'll try to explain what I'm doing as long as it ain't an emergency and I have the time. But, right off, I have an assignment for you. I want you to take the radio messages and write them down. If you don't understand the message, you can ask the dispatcher to repeat it, but I don't want you to do that every time, only once in a while, if you need to. Otherwise, if you can't get the message, ask me, but on every call, make damn sure to record the time, the code, the address, and the case number."

"Okay."

"We're unit 1113. Keep your ear tuned for it so you pick up on any call for us."

"My first FTO taught me to write our unit number on the back of my hand. I brought a felt pen with me, and I'm going to do that right now."

"Sure, Boy Scout. Whatever floats your boat—as long as you remember."

"All right, we're off."

CHAPTER 34

The First Call

"The first thing we're going to do is get some coffee. Until I get my coffee, lip from anybody will land them in jail; lip from you will get you tossed into the back seat. Just so you know, this is how I begin every graveyard shift; it's how I keep alert—especially during the middle of the night. You might find it helpful."

So, get your damn coffee, I thought. I hoped it would improve his disposition.

We pulled into a small parking lot next to Molly's Donut Shoppe. I recognized the store immediately because, in high school, we'd stop here for goodies on our way to the beach. There was a real Molly—a blonde, outrageously outgoing woman—who ran the place and made to-die-for glazed doughnuts.

"I also come here," continued Frank, "to write my reports, but I usually stay in the parking lot. As you can see, it's well lit, quiet, and safe."

We entered Molly's a little after ten. It was quiet. A few uniformed cops were sitting at high tops drinking coffee, and a few young couples were in booths munching pastries.

The cops seemed to know Frank and asked us to join them, but he declined, saying, "I've got a trainee in tow, and we need to go over some things."

One of the cops called out to me, "Hey, blue. Enjoy your ride with Frank." His fellow cops laughed. I thought that Frank must have a reputation for being tough on trainees.

When we sat down, to my surprise, Frank began questioning me. Why did I decide to become a cop? How was I doing at the academy? What were some things I learned during my last driving assignment? His interest in me seemed out of character, but then, I had been with him less than an hour. Maybe he was trying to assess how much he could rely on me. It led me to consider that perhaps there was more to Frank than the cynical, smart-ass attitude I had seen thus far.

We were back in the car and on patrol for about ten minutes when I heard, among other calls, the radio mention "1113." Then the dispatcher continued, "Twenty-three P at 1088 Grand, in front of Covi's Restaurant, case number 334871." I quickly grabbed my clipboard, but by the time I got the pen moving, the dispatcher had finished. Damn it, I wasn't getting all of it. I felt tense; I didn't want to screw up the first thing I was assigned to do.

"Did you get it down, Jerry?"

"I didn't catch the name of the restaurant."

"The restaurant is Covi's, c-o-v-i-s. Did you get down the rest of the stuff—time, radio signal, location, case number?"

"I did."

"Do you know what a twenty-three P is?"

"Well, I know that twenty-three P means robbery-person. Beyond that, I'm not sure."

"It usually refers to a strong-arm robbery. That means that the victim was physically attacked. Okay, respond to the dispatcher. Say, 'One-one-one-three, ten-four, ten-fifty-one to 1088 Grand.'"

I did. It was the first time I ever communicated with the dispatcher. My palms were sweating.

"Here we go," said Frank, accelerating the engine. "Whenever there is a robbery, everybody is suspect. When we get to the scene, pay attention to everyone. Watch everyone's hands. If the victims are present, I'll talk with them; you observe and take notes. By the end of tomorrow, I want you to be able to write our reports for the rest of the week.

"We don't know what we're going to encounter. I need you to watch my back. I don't want to be surprised. Your job is to see that I'm not surprised. You get it?"

"Yes, sir."

Arriving at 1088 Grand, we saw a middle-aged man and woman huddled in the restaurant's doorway. They were dressed up. She was wearing a blue suit with a bright yellow and white scarf at her neck, and he had on black pants and a tan jacket. It looked like linen. She was sobbing, while he seemed to be trying to console her.

As we hopped out of the car, Frank said, "Grab your notebook and write down everything you hear."

Frank went up to the couple, introduced himself, and asked if they were the ones who had been robbed. When they agreed, Frank shined his flashlight on them. It looked as though he was looking for cuts or injuries. Then he politely separated them and interviewed both, the woman first. He worked persistently at trying to get a description of the robber. Then he took his radio and issued a BOLO for him. He asked the couple to wait while he questioned the restaurant cashier and the manager.

Frank ended our meeting with the couple, a Mr. and Mrs. Ellis, by asking, "Do you need a ride home?"

"No, thank you. We're all set," the husband replied. "Our car is right there in Covis's parking lot."

"Okay," Frank concluded, "you'll next hear from a detective who will manage your case. He'll probably call you tomorrow. In the meantime, if you think of anything else that might help us identify the robber, please give us a call. Here's my card."

Frank and I then walked along Grand for about three blocks in each direction. Frank told me to me to keep an eye out for the victim's pocketbook or anything the thief may have discarded. We also looked for security cameras but found nothing.

CHAPTER 35

The Report

"Jerry, we've got no calls to respond to right now, so we're going back to Molly's parking lot to write our report."

Once parked, Frank said, "Before we enter our report on the computer, we're going to write part of the report on our notepads. You write your version, and I'll write mine. For now, you can skip the detail stuff on the first page—just go on to the narrative part on page two and describe your view of what we know. I'm going to try to get mine finished in fifteen minutes. See what you can do."

I grabbed my clipboard and started writing. About ten minutes had passed and I was halfway done when Frank dropped his report on the dash. He had finished.

"Let me know when you're done," Frank said. It came across as sarcastic. Talk about pressure. What did he expect? I had never written a police report before; I wasn't at all comfortable with the way this lesson was heading.

When I finished, I handed Frank my report. He quickly read it, and then, in front of my face, he tore it in two! I was so insulted and angry that I was having trouble mouthing words. Before I could say anything, Frank commanded, "Read mine."

When we first met, Frank told me that he wasn't a teacher; well, that was certainly confirmed in his response to my report-writing efforts. I was seething with resentment. However, by the end of Frank's third sentence, I saw, at once, the differences between our two narratives: Mine was written as though I was telling a story: "We arrived and saw a couple huddled in the doorway of a restaurant ..."

Frank's report began: "At 2242 hrs. we received a robbery call for a strong-armed robbery of a woman, Marlene Ellis. The theft of a gold necklace and small, hand-carried purse occurred as she left Covi's Restaurant at 1088 Grand Street, accompanied by her husband, William Ellis ..."

Frank said, "Look, kid, it takes a while to learn to write these reports. But here are a few rules: The report always has to answer the *what, when, where, who, how,* and *why* of the case. For most situations, that order will work. As you write, you need to assume that the reader knows nothing about the case. You also need to be aware that your report could end up being challenged in court; make sure you have all the key facts and be certain that they're right."

So, he *could* teach. I saw that if I could get by the shit he threw out, he knew stuff that I could learn. It reminded me of the problem I had with sergeant Gagnon until Don advised me to look past the delivery and focus on the message.

136

CHAPTER 36

The Inquiry

It was near midnight when we resumed patrol. The radio was eerily quiet. Not a call to any of the three cars working the graveyard shift. Frank was also quiet, driving the car and occasionally pointing out intersections that had frequent accidents or traffic problems. I thought that maybe this was a good time to bring up the question I had been wanting to ask ever since my one-day ride-along.

I started tentatively. "Frank, do you recall a case about two months ago when someone broke into a woman's house and messed up her panty drawer?"

"You must be kidding. Do you know how many radio calls I've heard?"

"I guess a lot. But I thought you might remember this one because the perp left a message on the woman's bathroom mirror that said that he would 'see her,' implying that he'd be back."

"Who was the detective?"

"I never knew his name. I just understood that a detective was assigned to the case."

Silence prevailed. It appeared that Frank was disinterested in my query. But after about ten minutes, out of nowhere, Frank said, "Why did you ask?"

"What do you mean, why did I ask?"

"What the hell do you think? Why did you ask me about the panty-drawer case?"

"Oh," I said. "I was involved with that call; it happened on my one-day riding assignment."

"Even so," continued Frank, "why bring it up? It wasn't a major crime, and that must have been at least a couple of months ago."

"I realize that, but I saw firsthand Nikki's—that was the name of the victim—fear and distress. I was just wondering if they caught the guy."

"Well, kid, I have no idea. Who was your FTO?"

"Jose Hernandez."

"He's a good, solid cop. Why don't you ask him?"

"I thought about doing that, but he's on a different shift, and I didn't want to bother him."

"You did the right thing, Jerry. It's not your case."

The remainder of the night was mostly uneventful. However, we had one call about a stolen private plane, but when we went to the airport and investigated, we found that there was no theft. It turned out that a mechanic had moved the small plane from the ramp into a maintenance hangar to perform some repairs.

CHAPTER 37

The Phone Call

My shift on Tuesday also turned out to be uneventful—many calls but all relatively routine. When we stopped at Molly's for our 3:00 a.m. "supper," Frank was his usual silent self, but, as I was beginning to learn, he was likely to drop a verbal bombshell when I least expected it.

As we were munching our pastries, he blurted out, "The detective was Anthony DeSota. They call him Tony."

"What?"

"The detective, the detective on the panty-raid case, his name is Tony DeSota."

"Oh," I said, startled. "You talked with him?"

"No," he said, "I just asked around."

My heart beat faster. Despite the hour, my sleepiness disappeared.

"What did you learn? Did they catch the guy?"

"No. As far as I can learn, they never identified anybody; it's on the back burner."

Instant ire. "It's on the back burner?" I shouted. "You know, Frank, he's still out there, and he said he'd be back!"

"Cool down, Jerry. Nothing was stolen, and the guy never returned. The detectives have more urgent cases."

I found it hard to believe that, for the two months since Jose and I answered the call, nothing had progressed. I wondered how Nikki was dealing with it. Was she still as scared as when I saw her? *Well,* I thought, *there is a way for me to find out. Call her.*

The next day, it was about noon when I awoke. I had gone to bed as soon as I got home from the shift (about 7:00 a.m.), but my sleep was fitful. Nikki was on my mind; I knew I wouldn't be able to relax until I spoke with her. So, rummaging around my room, I found the file folder of notes taken during that first riding assignment and retrieved Nikki's number.

Her phone rang and rang, and then her answering machine kicked in. To my surprise, the recorded message was delivered by a male voice. I wondered what that meant. Did she marry? She had a boyfriend?

"Hi, Nikki," I said to the machine. "This is Jerry Krone. I was the trainee with Officer Hernandez when your house was broken into and you found that note on your bathroom mirror. I'm back for a weeklong training stint and was wondering how you are and if there are any new developments. Sorry I missed you. I'll try again this evening, or you can reach me at 904-555-4893."

I called her again at about five o'clock, but once more, no Nikki, only the machine. *Where could she be? Did she move in with her sister?* I puzzled about it and then gradually started struggling to keep my imagination from conjuring images of her lying dead in her bedroom or maybe being dragged away by some rapist.

Fortunately, the need to don my uniform and assemble my equipment distracted me enough to temporarily put Nikki aside. But the concern kept creeping back whenever I wasn't distracted.

CHAPTER 38

The Visit

Wednesday night. It must have been around eight when my phone rang. It was Nikki. She explained that several of the nurses were out sick and that for the past few days, she had been working double shifts. She said that she was so exhausted when she got home that she didn't have the energy to return her phone messages.

"But," she said, "thank you for your concern. I'm okay. I've got an alarm system and double locks on the doors, but to be honest, I still get startled by unusual sounds in the night."

"I'm so sorry to hear that. Anything new on the case?"

"It's so disappointing. Nothing seems to be happening. No one has been arrested. In fact, they really don't have any suspects. I think the police have pretty much given up on it."

I didn't know how to react, but I felt compelled to say something, so I blurted out, "Why don't you call the detective and inquire if anything new is happening."

"That's a good suggestion, Jerry. I've been meaning to do that. I'll try to reach him tomorrow."

"Is there anything I can do to be of help?"

"Jerry, I hate to even mention this, but if you have access to a hammer and some nails, I could use a hand. Two boards on my backyard fence are loose. If you could nail them back up, I'd be so grateful."

I was so overjoyed by her request that I eagerly agreed. I told her that I could get to her place within an hour. She seemed very thankful and said that she'd look forward to seeing me.

As I turned down Seabrook Avenue, I began feeling uneasy, anxious. I thought it probably had to do with the prospect of my visiting an older woman—something I had never done. The tensions eased a bit when I mentally justified my visit as a response to a call for help, rationalizing that I was simply being a good neighbor, so to speak. Of course, the primary driving force behind my visit was to get more closure on the case.

When Nikki opened her front door, I was unprepared for what I saw. She looked older than I remembered her, but more than that, she looked haggard, tired. There were dark smudges under her eyes, and the crease lines around her mouth seemed deeper.

Her greeting, however, was warm. She invited me in and asked if I would like some iced tea or coffee. "No thanks, I said, "but I've brought my tools, so let's take a look at your fence."

We exited her kitchen door and went onto her patio, where there were two chairs, a lounge, and a low, round table—all in white aluminum. The backyard was small and grassy, enclosed by a wooden fence about six feet high.

The fence was constructed of four-inch-wide vertical planks abutted against each other and a top rail that held the planks in place. It was painted gray but looked shabby and in disrepair. The relentless Florida sun, wind, and salty air had eroded the wood, especially the top rail. Many of the nails holding the planks to the railing were popped out an inch or so, leaving boards loose and wobbly. Even the supporting posts were shaky because of rotting where they entered the ground.

At the fence's back left-hand corner, Nikki pointed out two boards that had come loose from the top rail. I looked and saw a foot-wide, V-shaped opening. We both peered through the aperture and saw her neighbor's house and backyard.

A simple job, I thought. A few nails pounded through the top rail into the planks, and that part of the fence would be mended. It wasn't until I lined up the planks, prior to nailing, that I realized, with sideways pressure, I could pry the corner boards apart, wide enough that someone could slip through the opening.

Nikki was aghast when I showed her. "Oh my God," she uttered. "Someone could get through that hole right into my backyard!"

"Wait a minute. Let's not jump to conclusions. I think the opening is too small. Let me try it."

When I wiggled and squeezed, I could only get my leg through the opening; it wasn't wide enough for my trunk and chest. And even though Nikki was tall and thinnish, it was indisputable that she couldn't slip past the open boards. But, I thought, someone who was short and slim possibly could.

I pulled from my toolbox a handful of sixteen-penny nails and in a few minutes had the opening closed tightly. We then inspected the rest of the fence, and where we found loose boards or gaps, I repaired them. Eventually, the fence would need to be replaced, but for now it was reasonably secure.

As we turned toward Nikki's back door, she once again asked about iced tea. I agreed, and she suggested that I sit on the patio while she prepared our drinks. Sitting there, I could see that the fence provided plenty of privacy from anyone walking or sitting at ground level, but that persons on the second floor of a neighboring house could easily gaze over the fence for a full view of the patio.

Nikki returned with a small tray containing two glasses of iced tea and a plate of Oreos (a favorite).

"Nikki, this is a nice yard. Do you come out here often?"

"Not much in the summer—it's too hot—but on most days off, when the weather is pleasant, I like to sunbathe and read. It's my way of battling stress."

"The reason I asked is that while sitting here, I noticed that your fence provides privacy, but in the house behind you, anyone looking out of the windows on the second floor can see right over the fence."

"I know. Sometimes I feel a little uncomfortable because I usually wear a bikini."

The conversation was becoming awkward; I didn't know where to go next, so I switched my questioning. "I remember how upset and frightened you were that night Officer Hernandez and I were here. Is that any better, or are you still really scared?"

"Jerry, it's much better. Thank you for asking. Right now, it's more a matter of frustration. I mean, we still don't know who broke in, and as far as I can tell, he's still out there; it's never far from my mind. But, as I think about it, right now I'm more angry than scared."

"Well, I'll be very interested to hear about your call to the detective. Would it be all right if I called you in a few days to hear what he said?"

"Sure. I hope I'll have some good news for you."

CHAPTER 39

Nikki's Call

"Detective DeSota."

"Hello, Detective. This is Nikki Wilson. You've been investigating my case. It's the one where someone broke into my house; I'm out on Seabrook."

"Oh, yeah. Has something new happened?"

"No, that's why I'm calling you. Is there any progress on finding the man who broke in? He said he'd 'see me.'"

"Ms. Wilson, it's still an active case. I told you that if something breaks, I'd be in touch."

"Yes, I know you said that, but I was talking with Jerry Krone, and he said he thought it would be a good idea to call you."

"Who said that?"

"Jerry Krone. He was with Officer Hernandez that night of the break-in—he's in training."

"That break-in happened a couple of months ago. How did he get involved now?"

"Well," said Nikki, "he was at my house last night, and we talked about the case."

With incredulity in his voice, Tony shouted, "He was at your house?"

"Yes, just for a visit. Is that a problem?"

In a voice barely controlled and filled with stifled anger, Tony replied, "Ms. Wilson, thank you for your call. I will certainly keep you informed about any new information. I've got another call, so I have to go now." A loud click told Nikki that the call was terminated.

The minute Tony hung up, he left his desk, angrily stormed across the detective's bullpen, and walked into the office of "Goldy" West, his sergeant.

He was called "Goldy" because several gold teeth were visible whenever he opened his mouth, and that happened often because he growled a lot. He'd been the detective sergeant for more than ten years, and he ran the department like a fiefdom. You didn't want to cross him.

Goldy's door was open, and he was at his desk. After two sharp raps on the doorframe, Tony paused for a few seconds until the sergeant pushed aside a report he was signing and beckoned Tony to enter.

"Sarge, you won't believe what happened," Tony ranted. "A trainee kid—Krone—is messing around with one of my cases!"

"Calm down, DeSota. What's going on?"

Tony explained that the kid not only called the victim but also went to her house and told her to call him to find out what was going on in the case.

"You're sure you're right about that?" Goldy asked.

"Yes, I am. I just hung up from talking with the victim."

"Okay. We'll put a stop to that. In the meantime, dig out the case file and drop it into my in-basket."

"Yes, sir."

CHAPTER 40

Trouble

The phone rang. "Gagnon."

"Anton. It's Goldy. Have you got a minute? I want to talk with you about one of your trainees. We have a situation."

"Who is it?"

"A recruit by the name of Jerry Krone."

"Really? Look, I can't talk right now. I've got a class starting in two minutes. How about coming over to the academy for lunch—I'm buying."

"Okay. See you at twelve?"

"See you then."

Before lunchtime, Sergeant Gagnon took a few minutes to review Officer Hernandez's training assessment report of Krone's first riding assignment. The FTO rated his overall performance as a nine out of ten, citing his excellent response to direction, conscientious effort, good rapport with the victim, and his eagerness to learn.

Hernandez's evaluation matched what Gagnon had observed at the academy—that Krone had plenty of smarts and was organized and hardworking. He adjusted quickly to the academy regimen; the sergeant also remembered how

Krone didn't flinch and stood strong when he accused him of sneaking into class late.

Goldy and Anton knew each other. They had been in the academy together and became sergeants within a year of each other. Both were old-school policemen who often disagreed but still respected each other.

After the usual catching up on families and especially their grandchildren, Anton got down to business. "So, what's up with Jerry Krone?"

"One of my detectives, Tony DeSota—maybe you know him—he's been around a long time, and he's the one that's as bald as a cue ball.

"Yeah, I know who he is; from time to time, he gives a few lectures at the academy."

"Well, he told me that your recruit Krone is messing around with one of his cases, that he phoned the victim and even went to her house, the crime scene. He told her to call Tony to find out what's going with the case. Tony's really upset. The kid isn't up to date with the case, and he's bypassing the chain of command."

"I'm disappointed to hear that. We certainly can't let this go on. Let's confront him and get it settled. Krone's on graveyard; we can meet him at six when he comes into the station off his shift. Can you make that?"

"Yeah," said Goldy. "I'll come in early. Maybe I'll have Tony join us."

CHAPTER 41

The Confrontation

As I approached the detective sergeant's office, I was surprised to see three men in his small room. It jolted me because I thought I was meeting with two sergeants—Gagnon and West. Peering in, I saw Gagnon standing to the left of the desk, arms folded across his chest. As usual, he looked formidable and angry. Seated behind the desk was Goldy, and in the only other chair in the room was a bald, older man in a gray sports coat, dress shirt, no tie, and brown slacks. He was scowling.

Walking into the office, I wasn't sure of the protocol, so I blurted out, "Oh no, this looks like trouble."

"This *is* trouble," said Goldy. "You might be about to be dismissed from the academy."

In shock and outrage, I shouted, "What? What's going on?"

Goldy said, "Tell him, Detective."

"It's very simple, recruit. You've been messing in a case where you have no business being. For God's sake, you're still in the academy, and here you are calling on a crime victim in a current, active investigation; you even visited the

155

crime scene." DeSota's voice grew in volume. "It's not your case. What the hell do you think you're doing?"

Goldy picked up the assault. "Krone, what you've done is bypass the chain of command. Anything to do with this case should be processed through Detective DeSota. How he works his case is his business. You're way out of bounds. If you were in my unit, I'd transfer you, but since you're not yet a cop, I'd recommend you be dismissed."

I couldn't believe what I was hearing. "Just a minute. I didn't interfere with anything."

Gagnon, who had been silent and standoffish, gruffly said, "What do you mean you didn't interfere with anything? Do you deny going to the victim's house?"

"No, sir. But—"

"But what?"

"I wasn't messing with the case; I was just following up."

I went on to explain that as result of two different radio calls, Officer Hernandez and I had spent most of our shift with Ms. Wilson in her house. We had gotten to know her, not simply as a victim but on a personal level as a woman shaken by the invasion of her home. I admitted I was curious, of course, about whether or not the perp had been caught, but my phone call to Nikki—the victim's name—was to inquire about how she was doing and how she was coping with what had happened to her.

"You told her to call me, to pester me," growled DeSota.

"No, sir. She had already thought about calling you. When I asked her if the intruder had been caught, she said that as far as she knew, no one had been arrested and that she wasn't certain if there were any new developments; she was anxious to know. So, it's true that I encouraged her to call you to find out what might be new, but as I said, she was already planning to do that."

"Tony, have you contacted Ms. Wilson to keep her updated?" asked Goldy.

"Sarge, come on, you know my caseload."

Sergeant Gagnon brought the topic back to Jerry. "So, Krone, what you're telling us here is that you were making a personal visit to this Nikki to see how she was doing and that you were not trying to get involved with the case. Have I got it right?"

"Yes, sir."

"Krone, we're going to discuss this situation and decide what's next for you. I'll contact you before it's time for your next shift."

"But—" I began to plead.

"No buts," Gagnon firmly intervened. "This meeting is over."

Given no choice, I walked out of the office. Angry and frustrated, I wanted to punch someone.

CHAPTER 42

Gagnon's Call

I can't remember being so rattled. I feel far more anxious now than I did nine years ago when I was awaiting my father's reaction to having punched Buzz. Here I am only a few weeks from graduation; it pains me to think about all the time and effort invested, for what? Nothing. And how will I explain it to my parents? Thoughts about the shame of being kicked out of the academy are unbearable.

I know that how this conflict ends will depend entirely on Gagnon. I feel certain, regardless of my innocence, he'll invoke some penalty for my contact with Nikki. I'm haunted by the uncertainty of how bad will it be.

I also wonder if Gagnon will check with Frank, my current FTO, to see if I spoke the truth about not involving myself in the case. And would he question Jose, my other FTO? I thought about the shift when we worked together. *Did I slip up on anything? Hopefully, both FTOs will give favorable reports, but even so, I have no way of knowing how the sergeant will interpret their comments.*

Well, I wasn't going down without fighting. *What can I do? I know. I'll talk with Don, my squad leader; with his*

159

extensive military experience, he might know the best way to handle this.

He had given his number to his squad members, so I called him, but there was no response. I left a message asking him to call me. *Now what?* I didn't know where to turn next.

As is true of many older teenagers, I often felt omnipotent. I had no need for God or religion. In fact, I had been questioning, Is there a God? Is religion just for old folks? But at that instant, for some unfathomable reason, I remembered how my mother handled crises. I followed her example and said aloud, "Lord, please help me." I was surprised how quickly and sincerely I turned to God for help. But then I also recalled how my father often said, "The apple doesn't drop far from the tree."

The afternoon wore on, but not a word from Gagnon. The waiting was nerve-racking; my palms were damp with cold sweat as I wondered if my career as a cop was going to end.

It was 1730 hours when my phone rang. "Krone, it's Sergeant Gagnon."

I could hardly breathe.

"Krone, you had a close call this afternoon—there's a fine line between personal discussion and case involvement. In this department, we follow a strict chain of command. So, next week, when you get back to the academy, you're going to read to the class the manual's section on chain of command. After that, you're going to be doing push-ups, all the while reciting, 'I will follow chain of command.'"

"Yes, sir."

"And, Krone, anything, *anything* to do with the Wilson case needs to be cleared with Detective DeSota. It's his case. So, until you're on active duty, stay away from the victim and the crime scene, and even then, do not do anything about the case without his approval. Is that understood?"

"Yes, sir."

"Okay. Don't screw up. Report to your shift tonight as scheduled."

"Thank you, sir!"

I never thought there'd be a day when I'd willingly say thank you to Gagnon.

CHAPTER 43

Working with Frank

The remaining four days of my riding assignment week turned out to be a tremendous practicum on police interactions—traffic stops, robberies, a missing person, auto accidents, car fire, officer's call for help, a beach drowning, and a domestic violence situation. Two of them provided extraordinary learning experiences. One was the domestic incident; it was a call that gave me a chance to perform as though I were a real cop, a heady experience for a trainee.

The call came in at about one on Sunday morning, the final night of my riding assignment. We were about to stop for a sandwich when the radio announced: "One-one-one-three, signal twenty-two at 1406 South Eleventh Street. Neighbors hear husband and wife screaming at each other. Case number 336152."

Since for the past two days Frank had allowed me to handle the radio calls, I responded, "One-one-one-three, ten-four, from South First and Cartwright Street."

As Frank hit the accelerator, my heart started to pound. I knew that this could be a potentially dangerous situation.

At once, Frank began lecturing in his tough, gruff manner, "Because of all the unknowns, domestic calls are one of the most dangerous, so two officers are always sent. We can expect that another car will be coming to the scene, but since we're so close, we'll probably get there first. If I were alone, I'd wait until the backup arrives, but since this is your last night of your riding assignment, I'm going to try to give you more exposure, but you must do exactly— *exactly*—as I tell you. Capito?"

"Yes, sir," I eagerly replied. I felt excited.

Frank parked the car a couple of houses away from 1406 and asked for the microphone.

"One-one-one-three, ten-ninety-seven at 1406 South Eleventh. Waiting for backup. We are two houses east of dispatch address."

The South Eleventh Street was a neighborhood of middle-income, single-family homes, all of which were dark, except for lights showing from 1406 in what probably was a bedroom. The temperature was a balmy seventy-two, and many residents had spurned their ACs and opened their windows. It was also eerily quiet, the silence broken only by the warbling of a few nightingales and the muffled sounds of the arguing couple.

"Jerry, we are going to get a little closer to 1406," Frank instructed. "When you get out, don't slam the door. Be as quiet as you can, and don't turn your flashlight on unless you absolutely have to. Stay behind me a few feet. We are going to listen from the yard of the house next to them. We'll assess things from there. I'm going to turn my radio down, but we'll still be able to hear calls. Any questions?"

"Yes, what would make us go in?"

"If the situation becomes violent, we move ahead. What we're trying to do now is use our time wisely while we wait for our backup. Of course, if it sounds like someone is getting hurt or killed, we can't wait, we can't play it safe. It's not always free coffee and doughnuts.

"Now listen, Jerry. When we do go in, we separate them. Here's how we'll operate: you take the wife; I'll take the husband. We'll maneuver them to opposite sides of the room. Keep them out of the kitchen. End up so that you're facing me. We watch each other's back. You get her story; I'll get his. Then we'll switch. Remember, Jerry, it's all about deescalating. Your mentality has to be that the police are here and we are in charge. Can you do that?"

"I think so. I'll sure try."

Frank led us closer to the house. We could hear snippets of conversation, "The house is a fucking pig pen," "You're so goddamn lazy." "You let the yard go to pot." And "What happened to our sex life?" The loudness and slurred words made it obvious that both had been drinking.

After a minute or two, our backup arrived. Frank apparently knew the officer and explained, "Tom, so far the husband and wife are screaming at each other about household issues, and we haven't heard anything threatening. I want my trainee to do a lot of this so he can get some hands-on experience. Is it okay with you if we handle it and you just have our backs?"

"It'll be a pleasure. Let's roll."

CHAPTER 44

Intervention

The three of us silently walked up several stone steps to the front door. Frank pointed to where I should stand (the right side of the doorway); he stood on the left side with Tom directly behind him. Frank banged on the door and shouted, "Police! Open the door!"

From inside the house, I heard a male voice say, "Oh shit." Then, after a few minutes, the door opened, and standing in the middle of the doorway, blocking our entrance, was the husband, a big-framed man but flabby looking. He wore a wrinkled black T-shirt and blue-checkered boxer shorts. I noticed that Frank, still standing to the side, was looking—almost staring—not at the husband's face but at the man's hands. I supposed that he was checking to see if the husband had a weapon.

Frank stuck his flashlight into the open door, about waist high, and said to the husband, "How about we come inside and talk with you and your wife a bit?"

"What are you doing here?" he slurred.

"We had a call. Now please let us in."

The husband hesitated for a few seconds and then said, "Yeah, okay."

As the husband and the three of us entered the living room, a woman came toward us from a hallway. I imagine it led from the bedroom. She wore a bulky white bathrobe; the hem of her nightgown was visible below the robe. Her hair looked disheveled.

As the husband and wife entered the living room, they scornfully glared at each other. Frank intervened immediately. He said, quite forcefully, "Okay, let's calm down. We're going to stop all shouting and talk this through."

And so we proceeded as he had earlier instructed me: Frank maneuvered the husband across the room so that when they stopped, Frank was facing me with his back against a living room wall; I did the same with the wife. Meanwhile, Tom stood quietly in the hallway at a spot that enabled him to watch all that was going on.

I began by asking the wife her name. She said that she was Wendy. *Now what?* I didn't know where to go next but fortunately came up with, "Why don't you tell me your side of the story?"

All I had to do then was to listen; she went off screeching about four or five of her husband faults (I learned that his name was Walt), but she kept coming back to his doing nothing to help with maintenance of their home. As Wendy spoke, the anger in her voice became softened.

168

When it was my turn to interview Walt, I used the same "Tell me ..." opening, but this time I encountered resistance. He said that he had already told the other cop (he must have perceived me as a cop!) what he was unhappy about and didn't see the need to go over it again. I explained that our report had to be signed by both of us, so I also needed to hear his side of the story. He seemed okay with that explanation and readily went on to tell me that he worked his ass off all day and expected her to work just as hard keeping the house up and making his life at home a relaxing one.

I couldn't imagine where we'd go next with this couple. *How do we resolve this call?* The shouting had stopped, but the air was still filled with tension. Frank once again stepped to the plate.

He called Wendy, Walt, and me toward a coffee table near the center of the living room. "Listen," he said, "we need a cooling-off period. You two need to discuss how each of you is willing to change to make your marriage work better, but you can't do that now when you're angry and hurt. You need space; you need to separate for tonight. Have you got a place nearby where one of you can go to—a relative, friend?" They both hung their heads; neither wanted to give.

"We're not leaving this house until we know it's peaceful," said Frank very firmly. "Peace won't happen with both of you at each other's throat. Tonight, you two need to separate."

To my surprise, Walt responded, "I'll go. There's a Hampton Inn three blocks over, on Route Four."

"I'll get the phone number, so you can check to see if there's space," said Tom as he radioed dispatch.

Walt called the inn, got a reservation, and went into the bedroom to pack toiletries and his clothes. Tom accompanied him. I remember Frank telling me during another house call to never let anyone leave your presence unaccompanied.

When Walt returned with his gear, Frank began concluding our call. He beckoned the husband and wife close to us and told them, "I hope you two can work things out. But it's not easy. Most of the time, couples need some outside help—someone to guide their progress. Here's a brochure for each of you. It lists all the local professional counseling services, including marriage counselors. I hope you'll give yourselves a chance and make use of them. Also, here's my card. It has my number on it and the case number. Mention the case number if you ever need police help."

We didn't leave the house until Walt left, and once he was out of the driveway, Tom, Frank, and I said good night to Wendy and returned to our cars. We had been there almost an hour. I felt exhausted, but I was smiling, elated because this domestic call further affirmed my decision to become a cop; it enabled me, once again, to experience the warm feelings and satisfaction I got from helping others. I relished the thought that police work had many more dimensions than enforcing the law or being punitive. What a night!

CHAPTER 45

At the Beach

On Thursday night, we had a different kind of experience. I learned that, while most police work is deadly serious, it also has its lighter moments.

Soon after we came on shift, Frank and I were patrolling the two miles of parking lot along the town's oceanfront. He explained to me that we were checking to make certain that the occupants of the parked cars, who were watching the so-called submarine races, were there because they wanted to be and doing what they wanted to be doing.

We cruised slowly with our headlights on and with our spotlight shining into the cars at the rearview mirror height. The light briefly illuminated the car's interior and gave us a good idea about what was taking place.

The parking area was well lit with sodium vapor lights that cast an orangey glow. It was not particularly romantic, but the parking spaces were only forty yards from the breaking waves. As we drove along, we saw two dilapidated pickup trucks parked near one end of the lot, maybe five to six spaces from the nearest car, their truck beds facing the

171

ocean. All the other vehicles were parked facing inward so that the ocean could be viewed through the windshield.

As we neared the trucks, we spotted two people standing behind one of the open doors. Leaning against the open door was a large woman (two hundred pounds or more), about thirty years old, with her pants and underwear down around her ankles. An even larger, shirtless man was behind her with his hands on her waist. His pants were also around his ankles. They were very intent on what they were doing.

As we drew closer, I could see his fat rippling forward and backward as he thrust into her. I thought, at the time, *This is probably what two hippos look like when mating.*

Frank and I were shocked. He stopped our car, but the couple didn't realize that we were there until Frank regained his composure and called, "Hey, you can't do that here."

The couple looked up at us in horror as they saw the police car. The woman, obviously the quicker of the two, quickly recouped and said, "We're waiting for friends."

Frank was not to be outdone. He immediately responded, "Could you please wait with your clothes on?"

With that, we drove off. Quite an experience for a young trainee, and quite an education for someone who had never seen a couple having sex.

CHAPTER 46

You Can Do It

Despite Frank's comments about his not being a teacher, I learned much during that week with him. While he constantly bitched about department procedures—especially reports and paperwork—his reports were always carefully written, detailed and replete with facts. He taught me how to craft a report that was not only acceptable to the department but, once or twice, brought praise from the sergeants.

Frank often complained about other cops on the force—especially about their laziness—but when we had calls for help, he unhesitatingly gave 100 percent of himself, once risking his life at a car fire. He taught me, drilled into me, the need to be thorough, to never be a passive observer—to be constantly alert to my immediate surroundings and to all the people in it—to purposely scan each car, each license plate, each person, each building.

Frank also taught me, by example, how to ask enough questions to fully understand each situation we were called to, even if it meant being a pain in the ass.

From a personal standpoint, I learned that while some officers prefer the graveyard shift, it was definitely not for me. I hated what it did to my sleep and how the odd hours made it difficult to be with those who worked normal hours—especially my family. I vowed that I'd do everything I could to avoid working that shift.

Driving home from my last shift with Frank, early on Saturday morning, I began musing about the past week. I found it hard to believe that I had experienced so many tragic situations. These experiences had a life-changing impact. Without being aware of the transition, I realized that I'd developed a tougher hide—an ability to encounter a crisis situation and remain reasonably calm.

The first time I recognized this toughness was at a horrific highway crash. It happened in one dramatic moment: We were the first to arrive at the scene. Apparently, an 18-wheeler had crossed the center line and had struck a small car, head-on. It could have been a BMW, but it was so demolished I couldn't tell. I glanced inside the car through part of the roof that had been ripped open and saw a man crushed, almost beyond recognition, sprawled across the front seat. His head was torn apart. I could see his brains and his eyes … Oh my God, I couldn't look. I felt my stomach churn. I was going to throw up. I turned my head and started to move away from the wreck.

I heard Frank shout, "Jerry, stop! Stop!"

I stopped.

"Jerry, think like a cop. What should you be thinking about right now?"

"God, I don't know, maybe the victims?"

"What about the victims?"

"How many? Who is hurt? Who is dead? Should I call for medical help?"

"What else?" Frank persisted.

"Look for witnesses. Look for tire marks—look for physical evidence of what happened ..."

The change was incredible. Frank had directed my focus away from the horrible scene and my queasy stomach to force me to start thinking, to do my job.

That I was able to dramatically shift gears in an instant seemed impossible. I would never have guessed that humans could do that. But there I was, shedding panic and starting to think objectively. It was more than how I was acting; something inside me also was different. I'd say it was a confidence, a confidence that I had never experienced before—the confidence that, despite any trauma around me, I would be able to focus on doing my job as a cop.

There's no question that I'm a different person today than that kid who, twelve months ago, decided to join the force. I hope it's for the better, because I don't think I can go back to being the person I used to be.

CHAPTER 47

Final Weeks

Time for our finals. Pressure had been building. All of us recruits—twenty-seven out of the initial twenty-nine—had long since qualified on the driving, shooting, and the defensive tactics blocks. Now we were facing written exams for academic stuff, like constitutional law, state law (traffic and criminal), patrol techniques, and a bunch of other courses. It was make it or break it time; fail an exam, fail the academy.

I thought I'd pass the exams because during the past six months, I'd kept up with the assigned readings but more so because Bridge and I had met several times to study sample exam questions. We knew our stuff. That wasn't necessarily true for all class members.

Not everyone studied; there were four or five recruits who often joked about skipping the assigned readings and homework. That day, when I saw them at lunch or in the hallway, their usual joviality and cockiness seemed absent; their downcast faces revealed worried looks.

These recruits were worried because failing any of the academy finals had a major consequence. Unlike bombing a college final where the penalty could be a failed course, at the academy, inability to pass a final defined a good portion of how you were likely to live the rest of your life; some of us would have police jobs, and some would not.

For me and Bridge, the academy's last two weeks were an upbeat time, a pleasant conclusion to six months of toil and pain: the goal of getting a badge was at hand, our instructors demeanor, even Sergeant Gagnon's, softened a bit—more like mentors then—and on Wednesday of the next to last week, we were issued official police uniforms!

Unfortunately, the uniforms were unwearable. While the shirt sizes were correct, the uniforms, fresh out of boxes, were badly wrinkled, and the pant lengths needed to be individually tailored. We were given a week to get them tailored and pressed and instructed to report to class on the following Wednesday for graduation photos, wearing the full uniform, "including your leather." We were told that under no circumstances were we to wear our uniforms (except for coming to class that morning) and to bring civilian clothes to put on once the photos were taken.

A few days later, the graduation ceremony was described: we would be called, one by one, across the stage to where the sergeants would present us with our certification and our badge.

We were also instructed that after the formal ceremony would be the pinning of badges. We were told to select, beforehand, who was going to perform that honor.

Along with the positive information, there was, however, a sobering moment. It occurred when the sergeants warned us that police station work would be a shocking contrast to the academy. They said, "Everything on the street is a lesson. Listen and learn quickly because failure to do so could mean a hospital, jail, unemployment, the morgue, or a combination of those."

Sergeant Dom concluded the uniform-issuing day with one last warning: "If you plan to go out after the graduation ceremony in uniform, absolutely no drinking. Remember you are now cops. Everyone will see you as a cop. If someone runs up to you and needs help, *you* will need to deal with it until assistance is called. From the day you get your badge, your life is going to be radically different."

CHAPTER 48

Fenced Out

Now that Tyler had located the bikini lady's bedroom and bathroom and learned that they both faced her backyard, he could hardly wait for an opportunity to peek into them.

His first chance came one night when his mom was playing poker with her friends and his sister was on a date. It was a dark night—moonless—a perfect time, he thought, to use his binoculars for peering through the fence opening.

Tyler had no idea what time the woman went to bed or even if the blinds would be open enough to see inside the house. But he had high hopes. He waited until nine o'clock and then ventured forth.

To Tyler's great dismay, he found that the fence had been repaired; the opening he had used to slip into the bikini lady's backyard had been completely closed. Worse yet, there weren't any cracks wide enough to look through, particularly with binoculars. *Shit*, he thought. All the good luck in finding out about her bedroom and bath had been wasted. He slowly came to the realization that he'd have to find some other source of stimulation.

CHAPTER 49

Another Victim

For Nikki, some days were almost free from thoughts about the invasion of her bedroom and bathroom. Today was one of those blissful times, but it didn't last for long. Her anguish returned with a bang.

It began when Nikki was having lunch in the nurses' lounge with her dear friend Dora.

"Did you see what was in the paper the other day," Dora said, "about the woman whose panties were stolen from her clothesline? It was in the police blotter column."

The coffee cup in Nikki's hand almost spilled. "No, no, I didn't see the article," she said. "My God, that's spooky. It could be the same person who was in my house!" Nikki's anxiety kicked in, big-time.

"Oh, Nikki, I didn't intend to upset you. Those notices are never current; who knows when it happened. Are you all right? You look pale."

"I'm okay. It's just that the thought of that creep still being out there makes me feel like I've been punched in the gut. As you probably remember, the burglar wrote on my mirror that he'd be back!"

"I'm so sorry I mentioned it."

"Don't be silly. Your telling me was upsetting, but now, as I think about it, the information also gives me a little relief. If this guy—I presume it's a male—is out there stealing someone else's underwear, then maybe I'm not his target; maybe I'm just one of many victims."

"I think you're right about that," Dora said. "I wonder if the clothesline lady got a good look at him. Do you think it would be helpful for you to hear what she has to say—you know, you two sharing your experiences?"

"You probably don't know this," Nikki replied, "but you and my sister are the only ones I've told about this horrible event. So, it might be interesting to hear what the woman has to say. I'm not sure, though, that it's possible to get her name or phone number. Don't the police keep that kind of information confidential? For the moment, Dora, I'm not sure what to do; I'm going to think about it."

CHAPTER 50

Graduation

July, in north Florida, can be as hot as hell. Today was no exception. But I didn't care. It was my graduation day. I hopped out of bed exuberant and eagerly looking forward to the 10:15 a.m. gathering of my academy classmates.

There was a delicious sense of excitement around our breakfast table; my dad took a day off from work, my brother was on school vacation, and even Mom seemed caught up in the celebratory atmosphere. She made a special breakfast of blueberry pancakes, maple syrup, and bacon—a treat usually reserved for our birthdays.

Arriving at the academy, I asked my dad to drive us around for a few minutes so that I could show them the campus and ivy-covered buildings. Neither parent had attended college, and I knew they were proud of my attending school here, just as I felt pleasure in showing them where I had been studying.

The graduation took place in the same building as our classroom but was held in the auditorium. When the chief stood and walked toward the podium, the auditorium quickly quieted down. He began the ceremony by welcoming everyone, and then he pointed to our group of blue uniforms and said, "These are a group of outstanding men and women who decided to commit their lives to the safety and protection of everyone in our community ..."

He continued on a little longer, and even though some of it sounded like the typical graduation bullshit, I concluded, from the many smiles throughout the audience, that his comments were meaningful to them; the families were pleased to be reminded about the noble calling of their sons or daughters. I also liked what he said but thought that it wouldn't be cool to let on that I felt that way.

The county sheriff spoke next and then came the mayor's speech, which, thankfully, was short.

Finally, the morning's most important moment arrived— the distribution of our badges—one graduate at a time. When my name was called, I can remember straightening my shoulders and proudly but nervously walking across the stage toward the first table. Once there, Sergeant Gagnon handed me my badge (with an engraved number reserved solely for me), and then he quietly said, "Congratulations, Jerry. You'll make a great cop." I didn't believe I'd ever hear those words from him; my huge grin was visible to everyone. He shook my hand and gestured for me to move to the next table, where Sergeant Dom handed me a leather folder that contained my certification as a police officer.

As I returned to my seat, I heard clapping from my family and Bridge's. I felt a little embarrassed, but soon the attention was off me as the next recruit's name was called.

When all the certificates and badges had been distributed, the chief had us all rise, and, as a group, he led us line by line in reciting the oath of office. It was a serious moment; the audience became hushed. The twenty-six graduates sounded strong as we solemnly made the pledge:

> I, Jeremiah Krone, as a citizen of the State
> of Florida and the United States of America,
> do hereby solemnly swear that I will support,
> protect, and defend the Constitution of the
> United States, the Constitution of the State
> of Florida, and the charter of the City of
> Fortuna Beach against all enemies domestic
> and foreign; that I will bear true faith, loyalty,
> and allegiance to the same; and that I will
> faithfully perform all the duties of the office
> of Police Officer for the City of Fortuna Beach
> Police Department on which I have entered,
> so help me God.

As I recited the words, "so help me God," it struck me how different this graduation was from the one I recently experienced at high school. That graduation scene was happy time—joking and laughter prevailed. It was like "Whoopee! We're escaping school."

This time, my feelings were different. While I felt joyful about succeeding in the academy, I didn't feel like laughing. I experienced more a sense of pride, the feeling you have when you accomplish something of significance. It had been a tough and demanding grind, and I got through it. But, I thought, more than that, graduation meant a commitment—a commitment to serve our town, to place myself in dangerous situations, and to be on call twenty-four seven.

So, mixed in with the day's excitement was a sobering, somber element. This graduation, I concluded, was a marker event in my life, an event that would shape how I would live out my working years.

Next, Don Scherer, our class leader, gave his last command. With great enthusiasm, he shouted, "Class of 2020, dis … missed!"

We clapped, shook hands with one another, and then quickly joined our families to get our badges pinned.

The majority of graduates were pinned by their mothers. As a family, we also decided to do it that way. Mom was not in favor of my becoming a cop, so as she pinned the badge to my uniform, I'm certain she had conflicting feelings. But even so, I believe she was touched by the solemnity of the moment. She didn't sob, but her eyes were wet. At that moment, I had an overwhelming feeling of love for my mother.

Dad rescued us from the emotional moment with a strong clap on my back and a hardy "Congratulations, Jerry. I'm proud of you."

Our family planned a celebration at home (many relatives), so I decided to remain in uniform. Later, Bridge and I were going out to celebrate; we agreed to dress as civilians.

CHAPTER 51

Celebration

I felt it in my bones; it was going to be one of those special nights. I washed and vacuumed my old Corolla and picked up Bridge at seven. Instead of coming out to my car, from her doorway, she waved for me to come in. She had a house full of family—two older sisters and a younger brother, along with many aunts, uncles, and cousins. I didn't want to go in, but of course, I couldn't refuse.

Fortunately, all were finishing up their meals around a large dining room table. I was able to escape having to think up clever small talk by remaining stationary near the entrance to the room. I simply smiled and acknowledged each one as Bridge introduced me. After a few "congratulations" and several "have a nice time" wishes, we were off.

As Bridge and I bounded down her front steps, we automatically grasped hands. I can't quite explain how or why it happened, but we seemed to be bonded. We had often discussed our enjoyment in being together, but this was something more. Making it through the academy and graduating together had unified us in subtle ways that neither of us had perceived.

We went to a place that had great burgers—Murphy's, a classic Irish pub. I didn't think it was a cop bar, but I'd heard that police often went there. We asked for a booth because it would be removed from the noise around the bar and made for easier conversation.

Almost at once, we began chatting about how, as rookie cops, life would be different for us. Would we be assigned to the same shifts? What would our training officers be like? Would we ever see each other on the same call? Did the department have any rules about cops dating each other?

We were so occupied with our exchange of thoughts I can hardly remember what we ordered. As the evening flew by, our animation grew. We both felt excited—thrilled with a let-it-all-out spirit; we were young adults about to begin a new venture, a new phase in our lives. We were flying high even though we hadn't had a drop to drink. We'd have to wait a few years for that.

With our arms wrapped around each other's backs, we walked through the dimly lit parking lot. Once in my car, not a word was said, but instantly we turned toward each other and kissed, tentatively and cautiously at first but then with desire and passion. This was as intimate as we had ever been.

The center console kept our pelvises apart, but we were both incredibly excited. *Where are we headed?* I was raring to go, but I had no condoms, and that small car was not where I wanted to make love for the first time. I had no idea about Bridge's sexual experience, but I was still a virgin.

During that pause in kissing, Bridge, still breathing hard, said, "Jerry, let's stop it here. I love you, but I'm not ready yet."

Immediately, and with pent-up enthusiasm, I responded, "Bridge, I love you too."

It was as though we had leapt over a huge chasm. Both of us spoke the words that we had been holding back, words we had not uttered earlier because we were afraid or unsure of the other's commitment. There was no doubt now.

CHAPTER 52

First Day

It was a tough night. I tossed and turned; I couldn't sleep. It wasn't worry and anxiety that was keeping me awake but rather the constant flow of thoughts about tomorrow and what my first day as an official cop might bring. Questions came rapidly, one after the other. Tomorrow, would I make any serious mistakes? What would my FTO be like? Suppose I had to fire my gun? Was it the right career for me? Had I aimed high enough? Should I have strived for more?

When the alarm went off at 4:30 a.m., I was already awake. From my bed, I could see my freshly pressed uniform hanging in the closet. After a quick shower and shave, I went downstairs for breakfast. To my surprise and delight, the whole family was there—mom, dad, and my brother, Bob. Still in their pajamas and half-asleep, they wanted to send me off with good luck wishes; Mom added a quick prayer to "keep Jerry safe."

It was still dark as I drove toward police headquarters for my 0600 to 1400 hours shift. We were told that for the first three months, every rookie would ride with a field training officer, spending one month on each of the three shifts. A different FTO would be selected for each month. For my first assignment, I was lucky, drawing the morning shift, but Bridge unfortunately got the graveyard shift, 10:00 p.m. to 6:00 a.m.

It was about five forty-five when I walked into the roll call room, and almost at once I heard loud sniffs. Then one of the assembled officers said, "I think I smell a freshly pressed uniform." Another commented, "I smell new blue." I had thought that once we graduated from the academy, the hazing would stop, but apparently that wasn't the case.

Ron had often told me about the importance of not being thin-skinned, and as a by-product of my academy experiences, I slowly began to acquire a tougher hide. In any event, I wasn't upset by the taunting and responded, "Good morning, ladies and gentlemen. I'm here to learn."

That silenced them, at least for the present.

At that moment, I was rescued by the sergeant who called out, "Are you Jerry Krone?"

"Yes, sir," I replied.

"Jerry, welcome to Fortuna Beach Police Department. I'm Sergeant Jack Mitchell. You're going to be riding for the next month with Officer Sam Jackson." Then, pointing toward a tall, bald black man, the sergeant said, "There's Sam, right there."

Sam appeared to be about thirty, with nice-looking facial features, including a bushy mustache. He was broad shouldered, strongly built, and looked to me like an ex-linebacker. He waved me over to where he was standing.

The sergeant stepped to his podium and was about to speak when Diego, a fellow academy student I didn't know very well, came running into the room. Glancing at my watch, I saw that it was exactly six o'clock!

The sergeant said, "Who are you?" (I think he knew exactly who Diego was since he probably had our two names for a few days.)

"Diego Sanchez, Sergeant."

"Diego, if you walked into an academy class at the same time the instructor was about to begin, how many push-ups would you have to do?"

"Maybe fifteen, sir."

"Well, here, ten minutes early is almost too late."

Sweeping his arm toward all the assembled officers, the sergeant continued, "In this room, we have the combined police experience of over one hundred twenty years. They all were here ten minutes early. Do you get the message?"

"Yes, sir."

At the conclusion of the sergeant's announcements, Sam and I moved toward the patrol car. As I had done as a trainee, I picked up the two shotguns on our way.

CHAPTER 53

My Show

Once we got into the car, Sam said, "Okay, Jerry, this is how we'll run your first month. Our work together is going to be called the Jerry Krone show."

"The Jerry Krone show?"

"Yes. I'll drive; you'll handle the radio and reports. For this first month, when we respond to a call, it's going to be all about you. You're the contact officer. I'm the cover officer. You'll work the call as you see fit. I'll guide you when necessary, but how you handle it is up to you. I'll be there to see that you don't get your ass kicked or get shot."

"I've never led on a call before."

"Of course you haven't. But even so, don't keep looking at me; work the call. If I see that you're struggling, I'll step in. Just remember, this is about getting you the most experience in the least amount of time. Jerry, you're going to make mistakes. What you learned in the academy are the basics. This is a whole new ball game."

Sam looked at me and said in a deadly serious tone, "There are a few things I want you, right now, to burn in your brain. One is that each of us is responsible for what we do here. What you do is on *your* shoulders, no one else's.

"Second, when we go to a call, remember we are the police; we are in charge. The type of call dictates the actions you take, but you almost always need to be assertive and, when necessary, aggressive. Try not to be demeaning or condescending.

"And finally, above all, pay attention to what's going on around you. Where you are, what people are present, what cars, what buildings. Scan, scan, scan. There's no such thing as looking too carefully.

"Oh, another thing. I want you to write the reports as we ride along."

"Sam, I'm not going to be able to do that."

"Don't give me that bullshit."

"No, Sam, I can't because if I try to write in a moving car, I'll throw up, right away. If you don't want puke in the car or on your lap, we'll have to find another way."

"All right. But if you are backed up with reports at the end of the shift, there is no overtime pay for rookies who are catching up on them. And as you probably know, all reports must be in the sergeant's mailbox so that they're available to him when he comes in to work. I'm not going to get shit for a bad report that you write, so this is what we'll do."

Handing me a business card with his email address on it, he said, "When our shift ends, you finish writing up the reports at the station. I'm not concerned about the check box items, but I do want to review the narrative part of the reports *before* you submit them. I'll be home. You email me your draft in Word format, and I'll send back the corrections I want made. You can then leave the corrected copies in Sergeant Jack's basket. Can you do that?"

"I can, but it looks like it will be long shift for me."

"Yeah, it will be until you can curb the puke or become a good report writer. In the police world, Jerry, you never escape reports; almost everybody hates them, but we all rely on them."

Sam started the engine. As we moved forward, the parking lot's electronic gate opened, and we were on our way. And then it came: my first radio call as a cop, a cop in charge no less.

"One-two-one-two."

As soon as I heard the "One-two-one-two," I recognized that the call was for us. I acknowledged, "One-two-one-two."

"One-two-one-two, signal fourteen at 13590 Sanders Street, case number 338729."

I grabbed my pad and pencil and started scribbling. I was still writing out the address when the dispatcher was already speaking the case number; all I was able to catch was the "338" part. I looked up at Sam, and without my saying a word, he understood my dilemma. He immediately told me, "Ten-nine" (radio code lingo for "repeat").

I keyed my mic and said, "One-two-one-two, please ten-nine the case number."

Without any additional comments, the dispatcher repeated the case number, and to my relief, I got the entire call on my notepad.

"Do you know what a signal fourteen is?" Sam asked.

"It's criminal mischief, if I remember correctly."

"Jerry, you're right." He looked at me with a wry, knowing smile and said, "Jerry, I'm the kind of guy that likes to jump in with both feet. Let's roll."

CHAPTER 54

Paint Job

Sanders Avenue was a short side street off Ocean Boulevard, a heavily traveled east-west road that ran from the Atlantic Ocean to I-95 and beyond. As Sam turned onto Sanders, I saw that it was lined on both sides with strip mall–like shops, each with a glass storefront and an entrance door. Between the street and the shops were parking spaces for patrons. The area struck me as being a bit shabby.

As we pulled up to 13590, I saw that it was a repair shop for small gasoline motors, like those on lawn mowers, leaf blowers, and hedge clippers. A Laundromat was on the repair shop's left, and on the right was a nail salon.

As Sam pulled to a stop, I felt a surge of nervous energy. I grabbed my notebook, ready to spring into action. I recalled Jose's and Sam's instructions about the importance of checking your surroundings, so I turned in a slow circle, looking everywhere. All was quiet—at 6:25 a.m., not a car or person could be seen, *except* for a short, middle-aged man standing in front of 13590, scraping paint off the glass storefront with a single-edged razor blade.

"Are you the person who called us?" I asked.

"Yeah, Officer, that's me."

It was the first time anyone called me "Officer." It almost caught me off guard; I fought the instinct to look around for the cop.

"What's your name?"

"Hans Hoffman." He had a slight German accent.

"Well, Hans, what's the reason for your call?"

"See for yourself, Officer. Some son of a bitch spray-painted my display window."

I stepped back from him and looked at the large pane. At eye level, someone had clumsily sprayed in bright yellow paint, STAY AWAY FROM MY WIFE. It spanned the entire window. Some of the letters weren't clearly formed because the paint ran, but the message was clear enough. Thus far, Hans had scraped away the S and part of the T.

"When did you first discover the paint?"

"Just a few minutes ago. I came in early to unpack some mower parts that I am planning on using today."

"When was the last time you saw the window without the yellow paint?"

"Last night, when I closed up, about five thirty."

As we were talking, Sam slowly walked up to within a few feet of us but said nothing.

"Okay," I continued, "I need to get some information. Please give me your name, home address, date of birth, and the best telephone number for reaching you."

"Why do I have to give you all that kind of information?"

I tried to reply without showing any impatience. "You called the police, and now I must file a report. Please give me the information."

I carefully recorded the data on my notepad, and then I asked, "Who do you think could have done this?"

Hans replied, "I have no idea."

"Mr. Hoffman, someone didn't write this message for the fun of it. There has to be a real issue here. So, let me ask again, who might be upset about his wife? Who is the wife?"

"It's none of your business," he gruffly responded.

Sam stepped forward and said, "Hans, you're right. At the moment, it's none of our business; no one's been hurt. But this whole thing could escalate. We need to know the players *before* anything else happens. So, you can cooperate with us or not, but remember, you called us. Why don't you start with who is likely to have spray-painted this message?"

"I'd rather not get them involved."

"They involved themselves when they did this. And you involved us, so now we need to know who the players are. If you don't want to cooperate, we'll leave. But in our report, we're going to indicate that you were uncooperative. If this guy comes back and burns your place down, I'm not sure how the detectives and insurance company will respond when they read about your unwillingness to help. It's up to you."

"Okay, okay," he said, sounding as though he had been beaten into submission.

Hans explained that he had been divorced for more than ten years and that he and a neighbor's wife had recently begun an affair. He said that he wasn't sure how her husband had found out about their romance.

"What are their names and address?"

"Hey, you're not going over there, are you?"

"No. Right now, it's only for our records."

I jotted the information on my notepad, and then Sam asked if Hans wanted to press charges.

"No way," replied Hans. "I don't want to stir up the pot any more than I have to."

"All right," said Sam as he handed Hans his card. "If anything else happens like this, give the officers the case number I've written here on the card. We hope you'll be sensible in resolving this situation."

I added, "And good luck with getting the paint off."

As Sam and I walked back to the car, he explained that my business cards were being printed and that I'd probably have them by the end of the week.

"Great," I said. I could see how useful they were for providing case numbers.

As we approached the car, I felt pleased. My first call as a cop, and I thought it went quite well. I knew that I'd hear from Sam about how I could have handled it better, but I felt confident enough to be open to his comments.

CHAPTER 55

Sam's Words

Sam started the car, and as we began to move, he asked, "Well, Jerry, how do you think it went?"

"I probably could have done better," I said, "but all in all, I thought it was handled okay."

"I agree. It was a routine case, but you took charge and collected all the necessary information for your report. Not bad for your first call; much better than I did on mine."

"But ..."

"But what?" he said.

"I was waiting for you to say, 'But, Jerry, you should have ...'"

"In the weeks ahead, there'll be plenty of those, so don't look for trouble. You did fine. The only lesson I have for you is this: victims and others at a call are often reluctant to give out information. I'm sure you can see why. But it is a problem every cop has to deal with. You ran into it with Hans, and I thought you persisted very nicely. Each cop usually finds his own best ways.

"When Hans was getting stubborn and I stepped in, you probably noticed that I was firm. Sometimes I find it helpful to provide a reason or two for wanting the information, but I never waver or equivocate. I tell them I need the info and need it now!"

That ended Sam's critique. But then he continued: "The radio has been quiet, so we have some time here. I'd like to show you a place that I find perfect for writing reports. If we don't get too busy, we'll try to keep your reports current so you won't have to put in a lot of overtime at the station."

"I like that idea. On my first riding assignment with Jose, he showed me his favorite place. It was the park on Oak Street. So, now I'll know two good spots."

"When we get there and you start writing, don't forget that you may have to drop everything at a second's notice. If we get a code three, we'll be taking off. That means you have to keep everything secure and organized, like your notes and coffee. Otherwise, when we accelerate, anything left on the dashboard or the seat is likely to go flying—a mess you won't want."

"I'll try to remember that, Sam. Thanks for the tip."

Sam's quiet place was one block off Mason Avenue at Foote Street. At that site, there was traffic noise from Mason, but it was quiet in the sense that the location was at an abandoned building; it looked to me as though it was once a supermarket. The building had a huge parking lot on three sides, but there was not a vehicle in sight. As we pulled into the parking lot, Sam drove to the rear of the building and backed in so that the rear bumper was almost touching its stucco surface.

"I like this location," Sam said, "because it's private; almost no car or truck ever comes in here. There's also plenty of space between me and anyone who might enter the lot and approach the car."

And so, with a wave of Sam's hand toward the computer, I began working on my report. I kept my notes securely on my lap and fed in my information. When finished, I turned the computer toward Sam. He read it, made a few minor changes, and said, "Okay, Jerry, call number one is taken care of. Let's get set for the next."

CHAPTER 56

Battleground

My first week with Sam zipped by. We responded to an incredible variety of calls—so much human tragedy—from indecent exposure to a deadly car accident. There isn't enough space to tell about all of them, but here's a call that occurred near the end of the week; it was sort of a baptism by fire.

"One-two-one-two. Signal sixty-three. Customer refuses to pay, China Grill, 1843 Morris Avenue. Case number 340514."

"One-two-one-two, ten-four," I replied.

When we reached 1843 Morris, I radioed, "One-two-one-two, ten-ninety-seven at 1843 Morris."

Sam stopped our car a few stores away from the China Grill.

"What are you doing?" I asked. "Why didn't you pull into the restaurant's parking lot?"

"I want to park in a place that allows us to approach the situation without being seen. I want to know what is going on—to see if anyone is armed."

"Makes sense," I said.

Sam went up to the restaurant's entrance door and peeked in through a small, round window. "Jerry, come here and take a look."

I peered through the pane and saw two people: a short, fragile-looking Asian woman (standing behind a large, old-fashioned cash register) and a huge male with a slightly dark complexion. He looked like someone from the Middle East. I judged that he was over six feet tall and perhaps weighed two hundred and fifty pounds. They were both waving their arms and pointing their fingers at each other.

Sam took another quick look and said, "It looks safe. Let's go in and see what's what. You take the lead, but I'll be right there."

"You called us, ma'am?" I asked.

"Yes," she said, pointing at the man. "He ate, but he won't pay his bill."

"The food stinks. It's rotten. I wouldn't pay a dime for it."

Sam intervened. "So how much of it did you eat?"

Before the customer could answer, the cashier interrupted, "He ate almost everything on his plate, and he also drank two cups of tea."

I recalled a similar case from our academy law classes and I said, "The law is that if you eat, you must pay for the meal."

The man looked me straight in the eye and shouted, "I'm not paying for this shit, and you can't make me." With that comment, he forcibly poked me in the chest with his right arm and stiff fingers. I was thrown a bit off balance and almost fell backward. Fortunately, my balance mechanisms prevailed and saved me from crashing to the floor. It could have been a nasty tumble.

At once, Sam sprang into action. He grabbed the man's right wrist in a wrist lock, forcing his arm up and around his back. But the guy was strong, and as he attempted to move away from Sam, he swung his left fist at Sam's face, connecting with a glancing blow. Sam's upper lip began bleeding.

"Jerry," Sam shouted, "code thirty-four, now!"

"One-two-one-two, signal thirty-four, code three," I excitedly shouted into my shoulder mic, desperately hoping that a unit would respond quickly to our request for help. Then I went to aid Sam. I knew from classes in self-defense that you should try to get the opponent on the ground, so I grabbed the flashlight from my belt and swung it hard at the back of the man's knees. He screamed in pain, and as his knees collapsed, he tumbled forward.

But the battle wasn't over. The man seemed incredibly strong and was still fighting Sam. I tried to grab his left wrist, but his constant movement made it difficult; his right knee then caught me in the groin. The pain was excruciating. For a few seconds, I had difficulty catching my breath, and I almost let go of him.

As the man made one of his backswings, I was able to get both of my hands on his left forearm. This hold slowed the customer down some, and it enabled Sam to get the man's right arm high against his back, forcing the man's torso and face down toward the floor.

I grabbed my cuffs and managed to get one cuff on his right wrist. We were then able to cuff the other wrist so that he was partially immobilized. For a minute or two more, the shouting and swearing continued, but the man must have gradually realized that he was losing the battle, and he finally stopped squirming. "You're under arrest," Sam declared.

"What is your name?" I asked.

"Shamir Kodda."

I now had a chance to look up from our battle, and the first thing I saw was one patron after the other running past us, trying to avoid the melee. We'd need some of them for witnesses, I thought, so I hoped they didn't get into their cars and speed off.

The sound of a siren and flashing red and blue lights announced the arrival of our backup. When the officer came through the door, he saw that we had things under control and immediately radioed dispatch, "Cancel the thirty-four. Subject in custody."

Sam knew the backup officer and called out, "Hi, Vince! Glad to see you!"

Quickly, Vince knelt down and helped us raise Shamir to his feet; he had now become quiet and sullen. The three of us brought him outside to Vince's patrol car, where we bent him over the trunk, facedown, and emptied his pockets. His wallet and key ring were all that we came up with. Sam patted him down but found no weapons.

I brought our patrol car up from where Sam had parked it, and we placed Shamir in the back seat. Vince said, "I'll stay with him; you guys go in and take care of your interviews and investigation."

"Jerry, get the statement forms from the car, and I'll meet you inside," commanded Sam.

When I returned to the restaurant, Sam had already started interviewing the cashier. I felt a tinge of anger; Sam had said that these calls were my show, but here he was taking over.

He had the cashier—a Mrs. Chang—print and sign the bill for the unpaid meal. Sam and I jointly interviewed her, and then, with a handful of statement forms, we individually interviewed the five or six diners who were still in the restaurant.

Finally, it was time for us to leave. We thanked Vince for his help and drove off to the city jail with our prisoner. On our way, I began using the computer to fill out our booking sheet. My first arrest; an experience I won't easily forget.

CHAPTER 57

First Try

Around the corner from his house, and one block over, Tyler had noticed, each school day morning, two teenaged girls waiting in front of their house for the high school bus. Their house was on the route that Tyler took when riding his bike from home to his junior high on Fairmount Avenue.

The girls weren't twins, but both were tall and lanky, each with long blonde hair that came almost to their waists. Usually, they wore tight shorts that showed off their tanned legs, but once in a while, he'd see jeans. Even though he rode past them almost every morning, they never said hi or acknowledged him.

Their house was a one-story ranch with white stucco sides and maroon shutters. It was easy to identify because it was the only house in the neighborhood that had a large chimney—a real fireplace. He realized that their bedrooms would have street-level windows low enough to peek into. There were also places to hide among the large hibiscus plantings surrounding the house. Tyler decided to look for an excuse to go out of his house after dark to see what could be seen.

Three days later, on a Friday night, an opportunity arose. His mother was going to the movies with one of her lady friends, and his sister was staying overnight at one of her girlfriend's. But there was a worrisome thing about the evening. His mother and her friend often stopped at a bar on their way home. She was unpredictable when she drank; it was at these times when her hairbrush was most likely to come out. She frightened him. The upside of the night was that the house would be empty until at least ten.

Tyler thought it was good that he could reach the girls' house without having to spend much time exposed on the sidewalks. He could go out his front door, cross the street, and walk in the yards between the Filmores' and Juarezes' houses to Sandhill Road, then turn left and walk a short distance on the sidewalk to the girls' ranch house at the corner of Williamson and Sandhill. The night was dark, perfect for prowling.

It was about nine o'clock when, with his Jaguar's hat pulled low, he opened his front door, looked carefully up and down the street, saw no one, and ventured forth. The scariest part was walking between the two houses on his way to Sandhill. What if one of those families looked out of their window and saw him? He decided that if he was spotted, he wouldn't run directly home but rather run forward and then around the block before returning to his house.

As he approached the teenagers' yard, he could see that most of the rooms were lit. Through one of the front windows, he saw the flashing colors of a TV reflecting off the walls in what was probably the family room. He figured that the bedrooms were going to be at the back of the house, so he started walking across the lawn toward the rear windows. Tyler's heart rate and breathing quickened as he felt the excitement build.

At the rear of the house, Tyler found two large windows, one on the left and one on the right, with a smaller one in the middle, most likely the bathroom, he speculated. Only one room, the bedroom on the right, revealed any light, most of it blocked by blinds. But Tyler immediately noticed light coming through a gap at the bottom where the blind was not fully lowered. He crept close to the window and peered in.

There she was, one of the teen girls! She was sitting up on her bed, talking on her phone, but she was covered, dressed in a large T-shirt. The shirt came down to her knees, but as she talked, she squiggled around so that every once in a while, the shirt would rise upward, revealing a quick glimpse of her crotch—enough to be tantalizing but not sufficiently revealing for his dick to respond. Tyler realized that the girl would have had to get undressed to put on the T-shirt, so if he had been there a bit earlier, he might have seen something more exciting. He'd plan another visit as soon as he could, but earlier.

It was frustrating for Tyler to be so close yet not see much. If he was older and had his license, he fantasized, he could get a van with big doors—like he'd seen on TV—and capture a girl. Then he'd have plenty of time to look at her—maybe even touch her.

Tyler struggled with that idea. He knew it was wrong and that he should stop thinking like that. But as Tyler battled his conscience, he found it impossible to conquer his compulsion to peek; he didn't want to give it up because it was so sexually exciting.

Heady stuff for a fifteen-year-old.

Heartache

Since our romantic dinner on graduation night, Bridge and I had only seen each other twice (for dinner or a movie and pizza). Our shift schedules made getting together difficult; even our days off didn't coincide. We had plenty of phone conversations, but they weren't like being together.

Today, as we neared the end of our first month of riding assignments, we had a phone conversation that I wish never occurred:

"So, Bridge, how are you? How are things going?"

"Terrible."

"What do you mean terrible? What's happening?"

"I don't know, Jerry. Maybe I'm just disillusioned. When it's time to go out on shift, I don't want to go—it's just too painful."

"Is it your FTO?"

"Oh, no. My FTO is Jose. I like working with him. The problem is what we're dealing with—the vomiting drunks, the drug addicts, the mayhem … the family abuse cases, little kids being beaten, a ten-year-old raped by her brother, the battered wives. Almost every call is tragic. It goes on night after night …"

"That's the midnight shift for you."

"It's more than that. The job is disrupting my whole life. I'm not sleeping well; I'm tired all the time. When I'm up and about, everyone else is sleeping. I hardly ever have time to be with my family and friends. And look at us. We've only been able to meet a couple of times in over three weeks. What kind of romance is that? This isn't what I expected when I signed up."

"Bridge, I'm so sorry you're having such a difficult time. How can I help?"

"I don't know that you can. I'm thinking about resigning. There are plenty of jobs that don't tear you up like this one."

"What about us?"

"I don't know, Jerry. You're catching me at a bad time."

Almost immediately, I experienced a sinking feeling in my stomach. What was happening? It sounded as though she had doubts about us. We needed to talk.

"Bridge, let's get together. How about dinner?"

"Not tonight; I'm too exhausted. Jerry, give me a little space, and I'll call you."

That sounded ominous. I was scared about what was happening with our relationship.

CHAPTER 59

Reactions

Yesterday afternoon, I received a phone call from HQ. The instruction was to report early for tomorrow's shift—0400! That was an order I had never experienced; I wondered what it was all about.

At 0345 and still not quite awake, I entered an unusually quiet roll call room. Sitting in the front row was Sam. He was chatting with three uniformed officers I didn't recognize. Not surprising, of course, since there were more than two hundred full-time officers in the department. Sam welcomed me with a warm "Good morning, Jerry" and waved for me to join the group.

He introduced me to the three officers—a Francisco Montez, Tom Rice, and Felicia Robinson. Immediately, Francisco mentioned that he was an FTO working with Sean Murphy, who, he said, was expected momentarily. "Maybe you know him from the academy."

I did know Sean; almost everybody did. He was a big Irishman with a large, round face and a full head of curly red hair. He was older than I was and had been in the military service. Sean was one of our squad leaders and was well respected at the academy. Just then, he walked into the room. Sean spotted me and said, "Hey, Jerry. It's great to see you. What's this all about?"

As soon as Sean appeared, Sergeant Donavan, our shift sergeant, who was standing at the podium (sifting through some papers), looked up at us and said, "Good morning, everyone. Thanks for coming in so early. The reason for the call-in is that today our three patrol cars will be providing backup to our department's narcotic unit. He went on to explain that at 0600 hours, the narcotics squad planned to raid a house in which their undercover agents had made several drug buys.

He continued to explain that our patrol cars would block the street to keep vehicles and pedestrians away from the scene, and we would also be on hand to capture any dealers who might attempt to escape the raid. He said that the narcotics squad's lieutenant would give us more information. *Wow*, I thought. *This is big-time.*

When Sergeant Donovan was finishing up his explanation, as if on cue, six members of the narcotics squad entered the roll call room along with a sergeant and a lieutenant. The narcotics team were all wearing street clothes, balaclavas pulled up on top of their heads (as though they were watch caps), and black bulletproof vests. I noticed that all were unshaven or had beards.

The lieutenant began the briefing. He told us that while no guns were seen during the drug buys, it was likely that the house occupants would be armed. If I didn't realize it before, I knew now that I was embarking on a dangerous mission.

As the lieutenant continued, he gestured toward the narcotics team who were standing in a crescent directly behind him. He looked directly at us and said, "Gentlemen, these are *my* guys. The good guys. Remember what they are wearing. Don't shoot them!"

It sounded humorous, but I could tell from his serious demeanor that he wasn't kidding. *But how are we supposed to do that?* I thought. They'll have their balaclavas pulled down over their faces, and except for one guy who was wearing a beat-up red shirt, their clothing was nondescript. Then one of the narcs turned his back slightly away from me, and I glimpsed at what would make positive identification possible: on the back of each of their protective vests, emblazoned in white, was the word *Police*. I didn't imagine that any of the druggies would be clad like that.

Then all the narcotics guys walked over to us, introduced themselves (by their first names only), and shook our hands. I felt awed by the meaningfulness of their coming to greet us.

Next up was the narcotics sergeant, Sergeant Clayton. He flipped a whiteboard over to uncover a diagram of a city block that showed four homes bordering a house that was circled in red. As he announced the address of the encircled house to be "4889 Boswell Street," he took a marking pen and wrote that address on his hand.

He went on to explain that we would travel to the address as a caravan: the two unmarked narcotics cars in the lead; our three patrol cars next. Sam and I were assigned to cover the front of the drug house and the house to its right; Francisco and Sean would be at the front and the house to the left. Bob and Felecia were to exit the caravan before Boswell Avenue so they could park their car on Sycamore, the street directly behind the drug house (to cut off that possible escape route).

After the briefing, Sergeant Clayton came up to Sam and me. He said, "I hear that this is your new blue. Is he going to be okay on this?"

Sam glanced at me and replied, "He'll be okay. We got this." I felt incredibly pleased at Sam's unhesitating support for me.

Before we left the station, Sam said, "I want you to cover the yard and house that's to the right of the drug house. We'll see if we can find some cover for you. I don't want to have to notify your parents. Understand?"

"I hear you."

During our drive to Boswell Avenue, Sam explained to me that, aside from being backup, another reason for our being involved was to provide a uniformed presence. This guarded against claims by the bad guys that they didn't know that the raiders were police.

CHAPTER 60

The Raid

The caravan proceeded unobtrusively—no lights or sirens. When we arrived at Boswell Avenue, it was still dark, dawn just breaking. The narcotics squad pulled their two unmarked cars directly in front of the drug house and ran toward it, guns in hand—four cops to the front, two around to the back. Sergeant Clayton brought up the rear.

Our patrol cars, lights now flashing, pulled up in front of the houses to the left and right of the raided house. The rears of our cars were facing the curb and angled out into the roadway to block the road and prevent anyone from driving by.

As Sam and I hurriedly exited our car, the narcotics guys, using a battering ram (euphemistically referred to as "the key"), were breaking in the front door, yelling repeatedly, "Police. Search warrant!"

Sam pointed to a large Florida oak in the middle of the lawn of the right-hand house. He said, "Jerry, take cover behind that big tree. If shooting starts, I want you protected; don't try to be a hero."

"Okay."

I was excited, revved up. This raid was entirely different from anything I had experienced thus far; it was scary.

From behind the oak tree, I anxiously held my Glock in one hand and my flashlight in the other. Suddenly, people were streaming out of the drug house. I saw two men jump out of a front window, but they turned toward their right, away from me. I heard Sam shout at them, "Halt! Police!" Then, from a side window facing me, I saw a man jump out of the drug house and run toward the backyard of the house I was guarding.

Speculating that he might be trying to make his getaway by running along the back of the house, I turned around from the oak tree and ran along the front lawn in the same direction I thought the subject was moving, toward the next driveway. When I reached the corner of the house, I stopped, peeked down the driveway (toward the backyard), and caught a glimpse of him at the end of the driveway. He was diving under a parked car; it looked as though it was abandoned and had been there for years.

I yelled, "Police. Police. Don't move!" all the while running down the driveway toward the car, gun and flashlight up. I wasn't thinking, just reacting. As I got to the car, I couldn't see him. I crouched, looked underneath, and there he was! I shined my flashlight and pointed my gun at him. Then, I screamed, "Freeze or die, mother fucker!"

"Don't shoot! Don't shoot!" he pleaded as he slowly crawled out from under.

As I was cuffing him, Sam ran up and said, "Nice work, Jerry. Here, I'll give you a hand getting him back to the car. You'll be happy to know that no one got away; they're all in custody."

Once our prisoner was securely locked in the back seat of the patrol car, Sam turned to me with a big grin displaying his bright white teeth. "Jerry," he said, "I don't think 'Freeze or die, mother fucker' is an accepted police challenge." We both laughed. I stood guard while Sam went to see if we could be of further help to the narcotics squad.

On our ride back to the station, I had a few quiet moments to reflect on my reactions during the previous hour. I couldn't believe I had uttered those words. I had never voiced them before. In fact, I rarely swore, and in our home, except from an occasional "damn" or "shit," my parents never used profanity. Today's gun-in-my-hand reaction helped me appreciate how adrenaline or emotions can override normal behavior and how police work can bring out thoughts you never believed you had.

The drug raid made me wonder, too, how I might react in a real gun fight. Would I be so tense that I'd keep firing away until the magazine was empty? The entire event gave me a greater appreciation for how traumatic it must be for the young in wartime combat.

During the postraid briefing, Sergeant Clayton pointed at me and said, "Good job, rookie. You got your man. I hadn't realized that the academy was teaching a new police challenge; I was glad to see that it works." He laughed. I sheepishly smiled, and deep inside, felt proud.

I hoped that the morning's encounter would help me to remain in better control during future armed confrontations. I'd have to ask Sam about his experience.

CHAPTER 61

No Response

I was so antsy waiting to talk with Bridge that I decided to call her when Sam and I took our coffee break (about eight), hoping that she hadn't gone to bed right after coming off her shift. I could hardly contain myself as I punched in her number. Her phone rang and rang until her voice mail kicked in; no Bridge. I ended up leaving a message to "call me as soon as you can."

I thought that perhaps she was sleeping and turned her phone off, so I called again during our lunch break, around twelve, but there was still no response. Why didn't she pick up the phone?

I waited until I got off my shift at 0200 and tried once more, but there was no reply. Anxiety flooded me. I could feel my pounding heart and my palms becoming sweaty. *What's wrong? Doesn't she want to talk with me?* Was there somebody else in the picture? Or did something bad happen to her? What was going on?

I couldn't sit still; I needed to act. I thought to call her mother to ask if Bridge was still sleeping, but then I realized that that wasn't possible because I didn't have her mother's phone number. What else? I could drive over to Bridge's house, but if I did that, it might look as though I were making too big a deal about her having a bad day. She might not like that either. *What the hell am I going to do?*

I decided to call Jose to find out if their shift ended at the usual time, 0600. He immediately remembered me from my driving assignment with him, so it was relatively easy to explain my concern. He told me that he and Bridget had a busy night, capped by a bloody domestic violence call in which the wife stabbed her husband, but that they ended their shift on time. He said that Bridget seemed to be a bit distracted and quieter than usual but not to the extent that it alarmed him.

My conversation with Jose settled it; whether it turned out to be embarrassing for me or not, I decided to drive to Bridget's house.

When I rang the doorbell, the door opened almost immediately; standing there was Mrs. Regan.

"Jerry. Thank God you're here. I just called my husband and was about to phone you. Have you seen Bridget?"

"No." I quivered. "I couldn't reach her on her phone, so I came over here to see if she was home."

"When she didn't come down for lunch—she usually does around one—I went to her bedroom to see if she was feeling okay, but she wasn't there, and, Jerry, her bed hadn't even been slept in! Right away, I called her sisters to see if she had made plans with them, but neither of them had heard from her in the past few days. Where could she be?"

My anxiety level was continuing to rise, but Mrs. Regan seemed worse. Her eyes were frantically moving left and right, as if she were searching for Bridget in the corners of the room. She was frightened; I thought she might collapse.

I knew it was not productive for the two of us to be so rattled, but what to do? Out of nowhere, I recalled having a similar panicky reaction after seeing a smashed body in a fatal traffic accident and how Frank, my FTO, got me back on track. Amazingly, that recollection triggered a change in me—seemingly, magically, I transformed from being an upset, anxious boyfriend to that of a cop on duty.

"It's going to be okay," I calmly said to Mrs. Regan. "There's got to be a logical explanation. Let's sit down and talk some. We'll find an answer."

"Sounds like a good idea. Let's go in the kitchen," said Mrs. Regan as she led the way, but when we entered the kitchen, she didn't sit down; she nervously paced back and forth between the entryway and the stove. A large oak table dominated the center of the room. The six chairs around the table, also oak, were cushioned, each one covered in a different brightly patterned fabric. The refrigerator door was nearly hidden by family photos held in place by magnets. On the countertop was a glass canister filled with large chocolate chip cookies. A cozy, homey ambiance prevailed.

"Does Bridget ever go to her girlfriend's place or run errands after work?" I asked.

"No, for the past three weeks that she's been on the midnight shift, she always comes home around six thirty and then plops into bed. I'm worried. She's never done anything like this before, and if she had a change of plan, she would definitely call me. Something terrible must have happened."

"I've already called the police station," I said. "I found out that Bridget finished her shift on time. I also learned that, in the past twenty-four hours, there haven't been any serious car accidents. So, we can eliminate that worry. I think Rita is Bridget's best friend. Suppose we call her; maybe from her conversations with Bridget, she knows what Bridge was planning."

"Okay, Jerry. I think I can find Rita's number. Bridget has a list of phone numbers on her desk."

Mrs. Regan took two steps toward the stairway when her phone rang. Nervously, she fumbled in the pocket of her jeans, trying to retrieve it. When she finally extracted the phone and held it in her hand, she glanced at the screen and shouted, "It's Bridget!"

CHAPTER 62

Dramatic Change

"Thank God you called!" Mrs. Regan shouted into the phone. "Are you okay? Are you okay?"

I couldn't hear Bridge's response because Mrs. Regan's phone wasn't on speaker, but I didn't care; I knew she was alive.

"Where are you? Wonderful! Jerry is here, and we can't wait to see you. I love you."

The instant Mrs. Regan lowered the phone, I jumped in with my questions. "Where is she? What did she say?"

"Jerry, first of all, she seems okay. She's at Saint Cecilia Church, at the convent, and she said that she's leaving right now. Hopefully, she'll be here in a few minutes."

"Did she say what she was doing there?"

"No, she only said that she was all right and that she's on her way home. We'll have to wait to find out what happened."

Mrs. Regan started to call her husband, and I went into the living room where, looking through their large picture window, I could view the street. I was tremendously eager for Bridge to get there, but strangely, another feeling began creeping into my awareness—a tinge of resentment. How could she not have kept in touch? Not a phone call, not an explanation for her disappearance. How could she do that to someone she said that she loved?

At that moment, Mrs. Regan joined me at the window. It was an awkward moment; I wondered if she had the same angry feelings that I had. I also thought that perhaps this was essentially a family matter, and my presence would only complicate a mother-daughter conversation.

"Do you think it would be better if I gave you and Bridge time alone? I could talk with her later."

"I don't know what to say, Jerry. I really don't know any more about why or how this happened than you do. Why don't you stay for a while and hear what she says."

It seemed as if it was an hour before Bridge's Beetle finally appeared. We probably had been waiting only ten minutes, but my anger and curiosity had me on edge. When Bridge faced us, I'd have to be careful not to blow it by venting my resentment.

When Bridge pulled into the driveway, Mrs. Regan and I didn't hesitate. We bolted toward the front door, ran down the porch steps, and greeted Bridge. Her arms were outstretched, and ours were as well. We met and embraced, the three of us bursting with emotion. Bridge's mother started crying.

Struggling to calm myself, I said, "Bridge, we're so glad you're home. Let's go in the house where we can talk."

After making one apology after another, telling us how sorry she was for causing so much worry, she finally was ready to explain where she'd been.

CHAPTER 63

Bridge's Story

Mrs. Regan led the way into their kitchen and promptly began heating water for tea. Bridge helped with getting cups from a cabinet while her mother assembled the cream, sugar, and what looked like homemade scones. *Come on, come on,* I thought. *Let's get on with it.* I couldn't wait to hear Bridge's explanation.

"First of all, where I've been these past six or seven hours was asleep. In a chair. At Saint Cecilia's convent."

"Now you tell us," I not so lovingly commented.

"Yes, Jerry. These past few weeks on the midnight shift have been murder; I haven't slept at all well. I can't remember one day that I slept anywhere near four hours straight.

"Along with the lack of sleep, the memories of what I've seen haunt me; I can't get them out of my head. They're so bad, Mom. I wouldn't want you to hear about them. One of the worst happened last night at the end of my shift—a stabbing. Nobody was killed, but blood was all over the place."

"Bridge, I find that I'm gradually toughening as I run into these awful situations. What upset me the first time seems less troublesome the second time. Do you think that might happen with you?"

"Maybe, Jerry, but it's more than the emotional strain. I just don't like the work. I still feel uncomfortable carrying a gun; I'm not even sure I could shoot at someone. And I know I'm never going to like working the midnight shift, and I'm not even sure being a cop is the right place for me."

"What do you mean?" I asked.

"It's all very subtle, but policewomen aren't seen as capable as the men. The stuff male cops say to me sounds like they're trying to be helpful—comments like 'Are you okay?' or 'Let me help with that'—but the way I see it, it's just a subtle put-down."

"So, then what happened last night?"

"All these thoughts were swirling in my head as I ended my shift. I was overwhelmed and exhausted, but I knew that if I came home, I wouldn't be able to fall asleep; I was too wound up. I needed a quiet place to think. I knew that Saint Cecelia's would be open early to prepare for the daily seven thirty Mass; that's where I went."

Bridge went on to tell us that, once in the church, she turned off her phone and sat in one of the empty pews to sort out her disturbing thoughts and feelings. She was quietly sobbing when Sister Mary Catherine, a nun Bridge knew from grammar school, came and sat beside her. They talked for a while, and then Sister invited Bridge back to the convent so that they could have more privacy and comfort because parishioners were gradually arriving for the Mass. After a long and helpful conversation, Sister left to teach her class, and while she was gone, Bridge said that she fell asleep sitting in a chair. It wasn't until about two fifteen that she woke up. Once she realized where she was, she called home.

I wondered if her epiphany at the church included the realization that she didn't want to be with me, but I avoided bringing it up.

"Are you thinking of quitting?" her mother asked.

"Mom and Jerry, I know you are going to be shocked, but out of all this turmoil, something good happened. I made a decision: I'm going to resign from the police department."

"Bridge, are you sure you want to do this?" I said.

"I'm very sure, Jerry. It feels right; it's like an elephant just walked off my chest."

"What will you do for a job?" asked her mother.

"That's something I want to talk with you and Dad about. I mean about finances and how much money Grandma left to me for college. If I can swing it, I'd like to go to college in the fall and get my degree in education. Off and on, for years, I've thought about teaching in elementary school. I'll never have to deal with that midnight shift again."

I was stunned. Bridge seemed to me to be well equipped for police work. We needed to talk.

"I know you and your mom probably want to talk. How about I pick you up around seven and we get a bite to eat?"

"Could we make it tomorrow night?"

"Sure, okay. Seven still good?"

"Great. See you then."

She took a few steps so that she stood in front of me, placed her arms around my neck, and gave a squeeze. I walked away, uncertain of how anything was going to go.

CHAPTER 64

Nikki's Torment

As Nikki opened her front door upon returning home from work, she heard her alarm system's now familiar "ding, ding." Then an automated voice said, "You have thirty seconds to enter your password." Nikki felt a warm sense of relief knowing that the system was still armed and that while she was gone, no one had entered the house.

As reassuring it was to know that her home was untouched, she still felt haunted by the realization that somebody had broken into *her* bedroom and, worse yet, rummaged through her underwear drawer. *Why my house?* she puzzled, as she had so many times before. *Why me? Is there someone after me? A rapist maybe? Some unknown, sick admirer?*

She thought there must be a reason why her bedroom had been chosen and not one of the hundreds in nearby homes. She knew that if she dwelled on this thought for even a few seconds, her curiosity about the event would quickly morph into terror; her heart would beat faster, and her body tense with anxiety. It was like having a nightmare while being awake. She wondered if she would ever get over those feelings and concluded that they'd probably bother her until the culprit was caught.

Nikki felt her anger rise as she realized that she had never heard a word from the investigative detective, DeSota. He said he'd keep in touch, but he never called her. She questioned whether or not the police were even working on her case. She wished Officer Jose and the young trainee, Jerry, were the ones in charge.

CHAPTER 65

Tyler's Route

Tyler had a great month. It all began a few weeks ago when the chamber of commerce sponsored a big weekend carnival that was set up in Central Park. It had a large food court and, of course, all kinds of rides, including a huge Ferris wheel. On Friday and Saturday nights, it operated until ten.

The carnival provided the perfect excuse for Tyler to be out of the house between nine and ten. He rode his bike to the park, but instead of going on the rides or meeting his buddies, he canvassed the nearby neighborhood for lighted bedroom windows. He found twenty or more, but most of them proved to be dead ends; the blinds or shades blocked him from peeking in, or if there was an opening to look in, the room was unoccupied or only revealed a young child or elderly adult. For Tyler, girls or youngish women were the sexiest; he had already discovered one at the blonde teenager's house by the bus stop on Williamson Street. Now, to his delight, he found two more windows that provided the views he sought.

It took Tyler a number of neighborhood visits before he determined the best time to be at each window. His system wasn't perfect, but eventually he devised a route that worked most nights.

The last stop on his route was almost always exciting. If his timing was right, his peeping would reveal a woman in the process of getting undressed. She was, he thought, in her thirties. She had small breasts but thick reddish hair at her crotch. It thrilled him to see one part of her body revealed after the other. But the show didn't last long; once she was undressed, she picked up a robe from a nearby chair and left the room.

Tyler was surprised how regimented and consistent the women seemed to be. Sometimes they undressed ten or fifteen minutes before or after the expected time, but usually he wasn't disappointed. During most tours, his dick got quite a workout.

CHAPTER 66

Code 3

What a night! Fitful would be an understatement. Questions kept racing through my mind. *What is going on with Bridge? Are we okay?*

When the alarm went off at 0445, it was a struggle to climb out of bed. But I did, and by six, Sam and I were pulling out of the station parking lot—the last day of my thirty-day stint on the 0600 to 1400 shift. On our way for the usual coffee stop, my hope for an easy morning was dashed when, at 0618, in came a call.

"One-two-one-two, signal twenty-three H, code three, shots fired, homeowner holding subject at gunpoint, 18840 Bayview Boulevard, case 241063."

With a nod from Sam, I quickly responded, "One-two-one-two, ten-fifty-one to 18840 Bayview."

We then heard another car (James, in unit 1213) respond, "One-two-one-three, I'm ten-fifty-one from Orange and Sixth."

Immediately, our sergeant (1210) announced, "One-two-one-zero, I'm ten-fifty-one from the station. Have all other responding units stay off the air until one-two-one-two and one-two-one-three arrive and advise."

The dispatcher repeated the command.

As Sam picked up speed and negotiated the sparse early-morning traffic, I could see an intensity on his face; it looked as though he were thinking something through. Then, half shouting to override the siren, and without looking at me, he said, "Jerry, Bayview Boulevard is in Sunshine Estates. It's a small, upscale development. Raise one-two-one-three and advise him that we will enter from the north; tell him to come in from the south entrance."

I keyed the mic, and as I repeated Sam's order, I felt the adrenaline dump. He said to me, jokingly, almost as an afterthought, "Can you imagine? A call before our morning coffee. Someone's going to jail!"

Then Sam shot me a side glance and said, "When we get to the development, you'll see that the lots are quite large. We'll stop short on the north side of the property and walk up to the house on the lawn; it's safer than using the driveway. And, Jerry, as we approach the house, take a deep breath, keep your head on a swivel, and think about crossfire. Remember, James is coming from the south!"

As Sam spoke, I found that listening to his controlled voice and his telling me what he wanted had an unexpected calming effect.

As we entered the development, Sam killed the siren and lights. We cruised up to the north side of 18840, and after he parked, Sam keyed his mic and announced, "One-two-one-two, ten-ninety-seven."

The dispatcher acknowledged, "One-two-one-two is ten-ninety-seven. Hold the air for one-two-one-two."

Her words were followed by the "hold the air" beep tone.

When Sam and I got out of the patrol car, we unholstered and moved together toward 18840. The house was a long, one-story ranch with a few lighted windows; the neighboring houses were dark. In the muted morning light, the house appeared tan with a red tile roof. It was absolutely quiet in the neighborhood. No one was about, not even dogwalkers.

We paused behind a large palm tree and then heard 1213's car driving up Bayview Boulevard from the south. When James exited his car, the three of us started to approach the house, and Sam, almost in a whisper, raised James on the radio and said, "One-two-one-three, take the rear from the south side; we'll go to the front."

James acknowledged, and we continued to move toward the house. Once again, Sam raised the dispatcher and, in the same hushed tone as before, advised, "One-two-one-two, dispatch. It's about fifty yards to the front door; this may take a minute."

I was surprised by how calm I was. There was so much going on, so much stimulation, so much information to process. I was simultaneously watching Sam, trying to stay clear of any crossfire situation, moving quickly, gun raised, watching the doors and windows, and all the while picking my way through the yard, trying to be as quiet and alert as possible. There was no time to think about the danger.

CHAPTER 67

The Entry

As we neared the house, James headed toward the rear while Sam and I each moved to a different front corner. Sam had already drilled this procedure into me during other calls. We moved slowly toward the front door from opposite sides of the house, staying low and quickly peeking into windows to see if we could learn any more about what was going on inside.

Once we arrived at the front door, we stopped to listen. "Don't move, or I'll shoot you again," a voice yelled.

"You fucking shot me!" Another voice. More bellowing and moaning followed.

"Police! Police! Open up." Sam beat on the door.

"The door's open. Come on in. I shot this guy!" The voice sounded excited, high-pitched.

"Do you still have a gun?" Sam thundered.

"Yes."

"Are there any other guns?"

The voice admitted, "Yes, but I kicked it away."

Again, from outside the door, Sam barked, "Back away,

put down the gun somewhere safe, and step back from it. Raise your hands."

"But I'm the guy—"

Sam cut him off. "Back the fuck up. Put the gun down somewhere safe, and put your hands up! Do it now!"

Sam motioned to me to push open the door. As I pushed hard on it, Sam peered ahead into the house and then crossed the threshold, heading toward the right side of the hallway. I carefully lowered my gun and crossed behind him, moving toward the left side (exactly as Sam had taught me). My reactions were becoming almost automatic.

We proceeded down the short hallway, guns up, lighting the way with our flashlights aimed ahead toward a dimly lit living room. As we entered the room, I saw a man lying on the floor moaning and holding his bloodied right arm. It was mangled and oozing blood. Another white male, with his arms raised, was standing near an end table next to the sofa.

Sam said to me, "Gun on the table, Jerry." Then he looked at the man with his hands up and asked, "Where is the other gun?"

"I kicked it under the couch."

Sam covered me, and I moved between the man and the gun on the table. When I reached the gun, I said to the man, "Get down on the floor." He started protesting, and, surprising myself, I loudly demanded, "On the floor now, damn it!"

Down he went, and, as per Sam's training, I cuffed him.

"Hey, what are you doing, cop? I'm the good guy. This is my place."

Sam quickly intervened and gruffly yelled, "Shut the hell up."

I heard Sam saying on the radio, "One-two-one-three, we are in, contact living room, two white males, and two guns. Come around and help clear the house."

Sam followed up with, "One-two-one-two, HQ, start Rescue. We have one male down with a GSW to the arm. We are clearing the rest of the house. Continue to hold the air."

James entered the living room, and Sam said, "Jerry, glove up and find a towel for the wounded guy to use as a bandage. James, cover Jerry as he searches him."

"Be careful. I'm hurt, and I ain't got no gun," he groaned.

I retrieved a large kitchen towel, handed it to the wounded man, and told him to hold it tightly against the wound. There was no spurting of blood, so I figured that there wasn't any arterial bleeding (something I remembered from the academy first aid course).

Sam and James broke off to clear the rest of the house; I stayed in the living room, covering the two men.

After a minute or two, I was startled when I heard, from the back of the house, a high-pitched shriek along with the voices of Sam and James. I then heard the sirens of the arriving Fire-Rescue units mingled with the renewed moaning of the guy who was shot. At the same time, the homeowner started complaining about the blood getting all over his carpet, and the wounded man angrily responded, "You shot me, you bastard! You shot me."

What a zoo!

I realized now that the man who had the gun was the homeowner; otherwise, he wouldn't be complaining about the blood on the carpet. I felt no sympathy for the man who got shot. I thought, *If you don't want to get shot, don't break into a stranger's house.*

Sam and James entered the room with a woman dressed in a nightgown, sweater draped over her shoulders. The nighty wasn't skimpy but revealed plenty of cleavage. She was tall, maybe 5' 10", and about forty, with short, dark hair that was disheveled and covered part of her face. She was obviously distressed; her eyes were bloodshot and still tearing.

When the woman saw the wounded man on the floor, she screamed, "Oh, my God!" and then she spotted her husband, cuffed and on the floor. She ran toward him, crying out, "John, are you hurt?" As she passed the wounded man, she kicked his leg.

"You bitch!" he yelled out.

I looked over at Sam; he nodded and waved to me to help the husband up. At that moment, the Rescue team came through the front door, so Sam and I escorted the couple to a wood-paneled room directly off the living room. It looked to be a home office with a large desk, bookcases, computer, and a small-screen TV. James stayed to guard the wounded guy.

CHAPTER 68

Yoga to the Rescue

As soon as we entered the office, Sam uncuffed the husband and said, "Sir, we are sorry we had to cuff you, but we had no idea who the players were or who belonged and who didn't. What we did was try to keep everyone safe. We're sorry it was uncomfortable for you.

"Now, though, we do need to ask a few questions in order to file our report. First, are either of you hurt?"

"No," they both replied.

"Are you the homeowners?"

"Yes," they said, almost in tandem.

"What are your names please?"

"John and Angela Young," John responded.

I could see that John was accepting our actions and understood the need for our questions, but Angela's face reflected nothing but fear; she was clinging to John as though she would collapse if she let go. In an effort to calm her down, John put his arm around her shoulders and drew her close.

Sam looked around the room and grabbed a chair for the woman. He looked at the couple for a moment or two and said, "I see a yoga mat. Do either of you do yoga?"

They both nodded. Then, in a calm, low tone, Sam said, "Both of you, look at me and please listen. Take a deep breath, all the way to your belly, hold it for three seconds, and then slowly let it out."

I watched in amazement how they readily complied. Sam continued, again slowly and softly, "You are safe. The police are here; the situation is going to get better. Now, close your eyes, if you can, and go to your happy, safe place. Take three deep belly breaths. With each breath, inhale the good, breathe in life; with each exhale, empty out all the bad."

When they finished and lifted their heads to look around the room, a change in the woman's face was evident; she seemed more relaxed and peaceful. John continued to remain calm. It was interesting to see how "tough cop Sam" could also be such a healer. I never knew he was into yoga.

"Okay, Mr. and Mrs. Young, Officer Krone is going to ask you for some additional information and get your statements. He'll be writing the report. A detective will also come to get additional information, and the crime scene unit will soon be here. But let's take one thing at a time and begin with Officer Krone."

Just then, 1210, our sergeant, appeared in the doorway to the office. He silently watched for a moment, nodded at Sam, and walked away.

After Rescue transported the subject to the hospital (followed by James in his patrol car), we reminded the Youngs that a detective and CSU would arrive shortly, and then left to finish our reports.

"'Go to your happy place.' Where in the world did that come from?" I asked Sam, amused and confused.

Sam smiled and said, "Namaste."

"What's that supposed to mean?"

"Namaste means that the divine light in me honors the divine light in you. We say that at the end of yoga practice."

Sam explained that he taught yoga and that these were yoga techniques for calming down. "I'll teach you if you want. It could be helpful for the rest of your life."

Changing the subject, he said, "We got screwed out of our morning coffee, and I told you when that happens, someone's going to jail. Well, this guy's not only going to jail, he's going to the hospital too."

As Sam continued driving, he smiled and said, "Jerry, you did well on the call; you'll do okay as a cop."

That was the best coffee I'd ever had!

CHAPTER 69

Now What?

I picked up Bridge at seven. I'd never seen her look so smashing. That's probably not the right word. Gorgeous. Feminine. She was wearing a short, sleeveless summer dress—whitish fabric with tiny flowers and cinched at the waist with a narrow stringlike belt. She was beautiful, and I felt completely underdressed with my T-shirt and shorts.

"Wow, Bridge, you clean up nice. After all that time seeing you in a uniform, you're looking fantastic!"

"Well, you have good taste." She laughed. "But yes, I agree. I *feel* fantastic. Now, where to?"

I was trying to think of a place that was not too noisy. "How about Duffy's Pub? We could probably find a quiet table there."

"Sounds good to me. I could go for a Reuben."

The ride there was full of small talk about my shifts and the routine banter of two people who enjoyed each other's company.

Duffy's was like many Irish pubs—dark wood paneling with a large bar running almost the length of the right side. Tables and booths were to the left across from a wide hallway that led to more tables in a small room at the rear.

The pub wasn't crowded, and we found a table in the back, away from the noisy bar. As we walked toward it, there was hardly a person in the pub who didn't turn their head to glance at Bridge. She radiated charm and beauty.

After we ordered, I was impatient to begin our conversation.

"So, how's your mom doing?" I inquired. "She was really worried when you didn't come home."

"She's fine now. She recovered quickly, once she knew I was okay. Actually, she's the one who suggested that we go out last night to celebrate my career decision. Along with my father, we got one of my sisters and my brother to join. We went to the Oceanside Steak House—a place we go for special occasions."

"I gather that your family was excited about your change of heart."

"I think they were relieved. They think my life will be a lot safer as a teacher."

"Well, I'm sure that's true, but …"

"But what?"

"I don't know. It's just that being a cop is sort of a special calling; the danger is a part of it. I couldn't imagine giving it up."

"I know what you mean about it being a calling, but it's just one that's not for me. Can you understand that?"

"I'm trying to, Bridge, and I do respect your decision. I think you'll make a great teacher, and you'll be happy because you'll be doing something you enjoy."

"Thanks, Jerry. It's important to me that you understand."

Then came a long pause, an uncomfortable gap in our lively conversation. Maybe we both sensed that the next topic could be difficult. But I couldn't wait any longer, so I plunged ahead and asked, "What does all this mean about us? I mean if I'm a cop and you're not."

"I've been thinking about that a lot. But tell me first, what do you think?"

"Bridge, for me, it's easy. I love you, and I want to be with you. If you're not going to be a cop, it's okay with me. But would it be too hard on you?"

"That's the big question, isn't it? That night in the parking lot, I said, 'I love you,' and I meant it. That hasn't changed; I want it to work out for us."

The rest of the evening, we talked about how we would deal with potential problems—me working midnight shift, where she'd go to college, having different friends (her college crowd versus the cop crowd), if she'd worry about the risks of my police work, if she'd have enough time for a relationship when she was striving for her degree.

We talked a lot, but not much was resolved. "Jerry, you know, we don't have to decide any of these things right now," Bridge reassured me. "Why don't we date and enjoy each other's company and see what happens?"

Inwardly, I sighed with relief. *Of course*, I thought. It was a way to go for us right now. With a big grin on my face, I stretched across the table and planted a kiss, right on her lips.

CHAPTER 70

Catching Up

She picked up on the first ring. "Hey, Bridge, guess what?"

"Come on, just tell me."

"At roll call this morning, the sergeant announced next month's assignment. For the first time, I'm to report to the West Station, and my new FTO is going to be Maria Martinez!"

"Is she young and pretty?"

"Don't tell me you're jealous."

"No." Bridge laughed. "I was just jerking your chain. Have you met her yet?"

"No, I don't know anything about her; I'll meet her for the first time when I report tomorrow."

"Well, good luck. I'll be interested to hear what you think of her."

"So," I said, "how about you? How did it go at your meeting with the sergeant?"

"It was so much better than I thought it would be. I was really anxious; I didn't know how he would react or how much pressure he might put on me to change my mind."

"What did he say?"

"First of all, he was calm. He said he was surprised at my decision because I had done well in the academy, and all my evaluations had shown that I was progressing satisfactorily. Then he asked me why I wanted to resign. I explained to him about the patronizing attitude of some of the male cops and how I detested the midnight shift. But I said those weren't the main reasons. I said that I wasn't enjoying being an officer and told him about my discomfort with guns—the fear that when the time came to shoot someone, I wouldn't be able to pull the trigger.

"He seemed very understanding but said, given my feelings about firing my gun, I should turn in my gun, badge, and ID today. He said he'd postpone sending the paperwork up the line for a couple of days. He suggested that I think some more about it, and that if I changed my mind, to let him know right away, and we'd talk about my coming back. The meeting worked out so much better than I thought it would."

"I'm so happy that it went well …"

"Jerry, I'm going to have to go now. My sister is having an eye exam, and I need to pick her up. She can't drive—eyes all dilated. I'll call you when I get back home."

CHAPTER 71

West Station

Fortuna Beach had two police stations: East Station (also called HQ) and West Station (often referred to as "the White House.") As the names suggested, East Station was responsible for the eastern portion of town, which included the ocean/beach area and extended westerly to the airport. It was the town's most densely populated portion; it was also the most affluent. Until now, Bridge and I had only worked from that station.

"HQ" was a three-story redbrick building that was once the town's high school. In 2012, it was completely renovated, and the police and two other town departments—Code Enforcement, Building and Zoning—moved in. All the police officials, including the chief, were housed there.

It was a little past noon, and I was on my way to the West Station for the 2:00–10:00 p.m. shift. During several casual conversations with other officers, I had heard that the White House was a fun place to work, that the absence of resident brass led to a more casual and relaxed atmosphere.

I'd never been to West Station, but I knew that it was near Cyprus Walk, a shopping center off Ocean Boulevard, about a quarter mile east of I-95. Cyprus Walk was a medium-sized shopping area that served the western part of town; it included a small mall anchored by Dillard's. Nearby were Walmart, Target, Lowes, and tons of small shops.

Except for a couple of new housing developments west of 95, the remaining area covered by West Station was sparsely populated. It was also low income. I knew this because, when I was working at HQ Station, I had to pass through there each time I drove from my house in Chesterville.

The West Station roads were mostly two laned, with many loops and turns. With few exceptions, the homes along the roads were unkempt; many yards were cluttered with abandoned lawn mowers, bicycles, and rusted junk cars of all descriptions. Tourists driving through the area would probably consider it trashy.

When I arrived at 2833 Black Bear Road, I got my first glimpse of the White House. I could see immediately how it got that name; the building was painted a bright white that made it stand out from the surrounding buildings and vegetation. It was long and narrow, with a flat roof. I turned into the station's U-shaped driveway and parked near the front entrance.

The front desk officer buzzed me in and told me where the roll call room was. When I introduced myself to my new sergeant, he immediately asked where I parked. I told him, "Out front."

"Okay," he said. "The gate code is 9272. Go move your car to the rear parking lot. Drive through the east gate. When you work here, always park in the back; it's the only way to be sure that your car won't be broken into while you're working."

I hadn't been a minute on duty, but the lessons had already begun.

Unlike the anxiety I felt when I reported for my first roll call, this time I was feeling upbeat and positive about meeting my FTO and looking forward to new learning experiences in that district. Thus far, I had been exposed to crime in an upscale area, but now, Sam told me, I'd learn what it was like on the other side of the tracks.

When I walked into the roll call room, it was an hour before the start of my shift. Standing inside of the doorway was a short woman with neatly trimmed, curly black hair that didn't quite reach her shoulders. There wasn't a hair out of place. She wore square-shaped, rimless glasses and looked to be about forty. She smiled, extended her hand, and said, "Are you Officer Krone?"

"Yes, I am. I'm Jeremiah Krone, but most people call me Jerry."

"Welcome to West Station, Jerry. I'm Maria Martinez, and I'll be your FTO for the next thirty days."

CHAPTER 72

Santeria

During roll call, the sergeant announced that I was riding with Officer Martinez, and he assigned us unit number 2312. I wrote it on the back of my right hand using a black Sharpie.

We pulled out of the West Station parking lot at about 1415, the beginning our 1400 to 2200 shift.

As soon as we hit the street, Maria began, "Here's how I like to work with rookies. During the first week, I'll drive, but after that, once you know the roads, you'll be at the wheel. As of today, I expect you to write all the reports. I have to warn you, though, I'm a stickler for detail. Accuracy is important to me, and you'll have to make it your priority as well. Does that present a problem for you?"

"I don't think so. I like things to be right; it's just me."

"Good. Until we get a call, I plan to acquaint you with this end of town. We'll start at the western border, a few miles west of I-95, and then work our way east toward the airport. There's a lot going on out here in the boonies, including meth and crack houses. I'll point out known problem areas, and it will be essential for you to get to know the road names."

All that first day and most of the second, we roamed the country roads without any interruptions except for a few fender benders and a bar fight we had to break up, including an arrest.

Now that I was in my second month, the paperwork was becoming a little more routine. I could see though that Maria had a writing style different from my other FTOs—more detailed and precise.

On my third day with Maria, on a late, cloudy, drizzling afternoon, a call came that would really set the bar high for strange experiences.

"Two-three-one-two. Signal sixty, reported suicide, 436 Fern Road, code three, case number 340746."

I quickly responded, "Two-three-one-two, ten-four, ten-fifty-one to 436 Fern."

Rescue also responded.

Maria nodded her approval of my radio reply, hit the lights and siren, and off we went.

"Jerry, have you been to one of these before?" Maria asked over the warbling siren. I was still amazed that officers could carry on a conversation, overriding the lights and siren, all while moving through traffic.

"No," I replied.

"Okay. When we get there, we'll need to move quickly and touch as little as possible. We need to find out fast who found this person and have them stay right there, but we also have to get inside to check if the person can be saved. Got it?"

"Yes."

We arrived at 436 Fern. I radioed, "Two-three-one-two, ten-ninety-seven, 436 Fern."

The residence was a dilapidated, one-story frame building with an overgrown yard. I noticed rotting boards all along the porch floor. An elderly couple, looking shocked and stunned, stood by the front door.

Maria called out, "What's happened here?"

The woman, gray haired, maybe seventy, wearing a shabby housedress, said in a hollow, low voice, "It's Carlos. I went to check on him. I haven't seen him in a day or so. I found him. He's in the shower."

"Okay, where do you live?"

Pointing with her finger toward the left, she said, "Over there, right next door."

"Please wait here," Maria ordered.

CHAPTER 73

Tongues

We donned our gloves, and, with her flashlight, Maria quickly pushed open the door. She yelled, "Police!" We entered rapidly yet cautiously into a small living room. It smelled dank and was dimly lit by a small table lamp with a bare bulb. Latin music was faintly heard coming from farther back in the house.

As we moved through an unlit kitchen, I could see that the house was unkempt—lots of dirty dishes in the sink, on the counter, and on the stove. The flies were buzzing around the kitchen like a squadron of dive-bombers.

We entered the bedroom. The bed was bare, the mattress stained, and the pillow greasy looking. The window was closed, and a torn shade was pulled down.

The odor became stronger as we moved into a dark bathroom. Using our flashlights, we both spotted Carlos. He was in the shower, semi-seated, hanging from a lamp cord wrapped around his neck and tied to the showerhead extension. His tongue was sticking out, blue and swollen. His jeans were tight, and his bare feet almost black from the blood and fluids that had settled in his lower extremities.

The smell of urine and feces mixed with body fluids was overpowering. Flies swarmed around Carlos; they were clearly interested in the soft tissue of his swollen, dark tongue.

What a disgusting sight. I got that queasy feeling in my stomach. *Please*, I prayed, *don't let me throw up*. I didn't want to come across as a wimp on my first significant call with Maria. Somehow, fortunately, I was able to hold it all in.

"Horrible," I blurted.

"Well, he clearly doesn't need Rescue," Maria deadpanned. "Speaking of Rescue, will you go out and see if they've arrived? And if they have, tell them that they can put their gear away. They'll want to come in to confirm that the victim can't be helped, so I'll wait here for them. And while you're out there, start getting information from that couple we met when we arrived. I'll be there to help as soon as Rescue gets in here."

Rescue got their information and departed, and then another patrol car (2314) arrived with my fellow rookie Sean and his FTO. Maria assigned them the task of putting up yellow crime scene tape and keeping the spectators away from the house.

After Maria and I finished interviewing the couple, we thanked them for their help, and then Maria said, "Let's reenter and go back over the scene. I want to point out some things that are important for a responding officer to include in any report. As you get more experience, you'll note these things on the first pass, but that will take some time."

As we were moving through the front door, Maria said, "Don't touch anything; just look and take notes." She spoke in a steady stream, and I struggled to keep up with her rapid flow of comments. "How did we make entry? Was the door open, ajar, unlocked, damaged? Who told us what was inside?"

She continued, "The victim is Spanish, maybe Cuban. I saw a red-and-white beaded bracelet on his wrist. Jerry, look behind the front door."

I peered around the door and was startled. On a small, wobbly table was a statue, incense, and a glass of water with coins in it.

With a knowing smile, Maria said, "Welcome to Santeria."

"What the hell is that?"

"It's a religion. That statue there is Santa Barbara, a Santeria deity. Her colors are red and white. See the incense? I smelled it on the way in. The glass in front of the statue is filled with water, and the coins are an offering. The candle is a homage. When you describe it in your report, say it's a clear liquid; you don't know if it's water or not. You could drink it to find out, but I wouldn't suggest that. Just note all that you see. This is the kind of stuff that will set your reports apart from others who are too lazy to be thorough."

I immediately appreciated Maria's ability as a trainer. This one call gave me a new structure for managing my calls.

"Come on, Jerry. Let's move into the kitchen. Do you see any signs of struggle, knives, or any weapons? What do you see?"

As I slowly looked around the small kitchen, I was startled again; a cow's tongue was half-hidden by a piece of newspaper wrapped in string with toothpicks sticking out of it.

"Jerry, when the ME gets here, he will collect that too. I bet it's got the victim's name on it. For now, in your report, note the tongue and its location."

I felt shocked. I had never heard of or seen anything like this.

Next, we moved into the bedroom, and Maria asked, "What do you see here?"

"I see another candle."

"What's on the candle?"

"An old man with dogs."

"That's Saint Lazaro. He's another Santeria deity, a god. Orisha is the word they use. He's the deity for health, sickness, love, and fear. My guess is that fear has a part in this. Jerry, be sure to note the candle.

"Any sign of a struggle?"

"No, but this place is a filthy mess."

"Exactly. We'll note that in the report. I'll tell you how to phrase it."

"Let's look at the body."

We walked into the bathroom. This was the moment I was dreading. Would I be able to manage the sight? Could

I keep my stomach in control one more time? I wanted to turn my head away.

She must have noticed my reluctance to step close to the body, as she said, "Focus, Jerry. He can't hurt anyone. He's just hanging around! The sooner we get this done, the sooner we're out of here. I'll tell you what to look at. You take the notes.

"What's the cord that he has wrapped around his neck made of? What's it attached to?

"Describe the body position and which way it faces. I would say, for example, facing south, semi-kneeling, unbound hands at his side.

"Where's the knot located?

"What's the victim wearing? What clothing is missing?

"Is he wearing any jewelry?

"Describe the wristlet."

"I'm trying to get it written down."

I probably sounded a bit overwhelmed. I think Maria sensed this. She said, "Jerry, we'll go over all this when we get back to the car. Just write down the items I tell you about, and I'll help you sort through everything later.

"Anyway, I think we're about done, except for one thing. He's hanging from an electrical cord of some type. On the way out, look for something that's missing a cord. If we don't find one, it paints a whole other picture. Whatever you find or don't find, note that too."

I was so relieved to be out of the house. I had never been in a place like that.

"Jerry, it may take a while before homicide gets here, so we'll go to the car and start on the report."

We had only been working for about ten minutes when an unmarked car pulled in alongside of us and a tall, casually dressed man came to our car. He greeted Maria and said to me, "Hello, Officer. I'm Detective Juan Garcia. What have we got here, Maria?"

Apparently, Maria and Juan knew each other. She briefed him on our findings, and after a quick thanks, he departed and entered the house. Maria then turned toward me and surprised me by saying, "So, let's finish things up. I'm getting hungry. I know a great Italian place not too far from here. We can eat and finish up your report there."

Eating was definitely not on my mind, but I didn't want to be seen as a wuss, so I enthusiastically replied, "Sure, let's go."

CHAPTER 74

Crawl Space

For the next three weeks, Maria and I had lots of calls, many of which were new to me—calls that were common for the West Station but rarely encountered out of the East—like reports of stolen lawn mowers and farm gear and even the torching of abandoned shacks.

While not unique to West Station, we had quite a few domestics. I had never realized that families argued so much and called the police to resolve the issues. I went home one night and told my family about a mother who called the police because her twelve-year-old son said that he wasn't going to do his homework!

Another call, not so mundane, revealed a part of Maria's personality I had not seen before. It happened one night, soon after dark, when we received a signal twenty-four about a man hiding under a house. When we arrived at the location, the house turned out to be a small, two-bedroom cottage. It looked a bit seedy. The upper half was painted a dark blue, while the lower part was a white—well, let's say, a grayish white. The paint was faded and peeling in many spots. Overall, the building struck me as run-down.

No sooner had we parked the car than a middle-aged man and woman ran from the house to greet us. They appeared rattled and upset, explaining that a man was in the crawl space underneath their home.

"He's screaming like he's in battle," the woman said in a trembling, high-pitched voice.

"Yeah," added the husband. "He was shouting that he was surrounded and to not let the Iraqis get him!"

We could hear the man's muffled screams, even from where we were standing at the curb. Maria instructed the couple to remain near the patrol car and then said to me, "Jerry, stay close, watch my six, and when we make contact, keep an eye on his hands. We're going to approach the house but stay away from the air vents in the foundation. Let's see if we can talk with this guy. I think he's having a flashback."

We then heard a helicopter approaching. Its Nightsun spotlight came on and flashed around the neighborhood as it circled above. At the same time, our backup officer also arrived. Maria knew him—Marcus—and asked him to watch the front and the other side of the house while we made our way, on the near side, heading toward the rear.

As we were moved along the yard, Maria contacted the guy in the sheriff's copter and asked him to "stick around but to back off about a mile."

I heard his terse reply, "Ten-four, ma'am," and then he moved off a bit.

When we neared the rear of the home, I could see now that the house was set on a solid, concrete foundation, rising perhaps a couple of feet above the ground. An entrance to the crawl space, at the back, was provided by a narrow opening in the foundation. I didn't see any door, although I imagined that, originally, there was one. To access the crawl space, two slabs of concrete served as steps leading down to the opening. If someone wanted to go farther under the house, they'd have to crawl on their hands and knees.

CHAPTER 75

Jessup

Maria drew her gun, and I followed her lead. While we had flashlights, we didn't turn them on, relying instead, on the neighborhood's ambient light. We both stood next to the opening, me with my back against the house (so I could look in three directions), while Maria faced the entrance.

She called through the opening, "Brother, they're gone. We beat them back. Hear the dust-off? It's circling the LZ to get the wounded. We need to un-ass this place before a counterattack. So, let's go, soldier. We ain't waiting all day for you."

No response.

Maria continued, "Soldier, what's your name?"

"Jessup." It was so weakly spoken that I could hardly hear him.

Maria tried again. "Okay, Jessup, we need to go. We got medics to check you. No one's going to hurt you. All the bad guys are gone, I promise. Come on, Jessup. Let's go home."

I heard some metallic clinking, and Maria said, "Jessup, leave your gear and just come out from under there."

"I'm coming. Don't let them leave me!"

"No one's gonna leave you. We got you, man. Come on, brother, you can do it."

I could hear Jessup crawling through whatever debris was in the crawl space. Maria peered in the entrance, trying to spot him. As he slowly crawled toward us, we first saw his head and gradually the rest of his body. I could see that his hands were empty. We each grasped an arm and helped him up the two steps.

"You got anything on you, man?"

Silence.

"Jerry, pat him down." Then she said, "Jessup, my name is Maria. How about we get out of here? You're safe." She gently put her hand on his shoulder and said, "You're okay, man. You had a bad dream. You're safe; we're here to help you."

Jessup was a black man covered with patches of sandy soil from under the house. I judged him to be about fifty. He was also a little glassy-eyed.

As we walked toward the patrol car, Maria continued to speak in calm, even tones, asking questions like "You know where you are? Where do you stay?" Gradually, she got a few responses. It was obvious that Jessup was coming down from a high of some sort, one that may have caused the flashback.

As we walked, Maria got on the radio and advised the chopper that the situation was resolved. Again, the pilot responded, "Ten-four," and flew off. She then turned her attention to Jessup and said, "We're going to take you to talk to someone, but we have to handcuff you in the car till we get there. That okay?"

"Okay."

I gently cuffed him. He seemed familiar with this routine. We brushed the dust off his clothes, placed him in the patrol car, and drove him to the VA Crisis Center that was out in the county.

On our way back from the VA, I thought about my earlier perceptions of Maria. With her focus on accuracy and fussiness about details, she often seemed cold and unemotional. But that evening, I saw an entirely different Maria—one who was compassionate and caring. I was amazed, too, at how adaptive and flexible she was, speaking the vet's language to entice him out of that crawl space.

I told Maria that I noticed the reassuring monologue she maintained as she guided the vet out of the crawl space. "Where did you learn how to do that?" I asked.

Maria told me that she was a Gulf War vet, a marine, and that she understood the flashback thing. She said that some people don't ever really come back and move on; it's like they can't get away from their past. Then she said, "Remember, Jerry, in this job, everything that you know, everything that you are or want to be, can be a tool in your toolbox; that's what's so great about this job. It's always changing and always challenging."

As we sat quietly and I wrote the report, I realized how fortunate I was to have Maria as an FTO.

CHAPTER 76

Detective's Comments

A good thing happened to me—a little praise. I couldn't wait to share it with Bridge.

It was about a week since we responded to the call for the hanging, and Maria and I were at Mabel's, her favorite coffee shop. Besides drinking coffee, we were doing what we always seemed to be doing, writing another report. They used to be tedious, but now they were much easier, largely because Maria had been a good mentor; she helped me learn what I should observe and how to best phrase my findings.

On our portable radio, we heard, "Unit thirty-one, HQ."

"HQ, thirty-one."

"HQ, thirty-one. Will you please have unit two-three-one-two advise on their ten-twenty. I need to speak with them."

"What do you suppose that's all about?" I asked Maria.

"I don't know, Jerry. That's Juan Garcia, the detective we met at the hanging."

After HQ radioed us and we replied with our ten-twenty, we heard, "Two-three-one-two. Thirty-one. Ten minutes. Ten-four."

A few minutes later, Garcia strolled in. I was immediately struck by his cocky demeanor—his swagger and the way he dressed. He had on a white dress shirt with an open collar, and his cuffs were turned up. Expensive-looking jeans and fancy, low boots completed the outfit. With his clean-shaven face and square-jawed chin, he looked imposing; I could see how women might find him attractive.

I was in the middle of writing up a call when he approached our table. He smiled, looked at Maria, and said, "Well, I see that some things don't change. How many rookies have you brought here to tune up their reports? This table should have your name on it!"

"Thanks, Juan. Teaching report writing is never-ending—some take longer than others. Jerry, here, is doing okay, but I limit the compliments; he's still new blue."

Garcia extended his arm to shake my hand and said, "Glad to see you again. I've read that hanging report many times. The reason I called is that I thought you two might be interested in hearing the rest of the story about the hanging. But first, who wrote the report?"

Maria responded, "Jerry. It was his first hanging. I advised."

"I figured; the style looked familiar. You did a nice job. You know, Jerry, Maria always prepares a great report; her attention to detail is the best you'll find. If you can absorb what she says, it'll pay off in your career, and all the details you record will be really helpful when you go to court, especially if a trial comes up years after you've written them.

"So, anyway, getting back to the rest of the story, it seems that our victim was a snitch working with the feds. From what I can gather, he was a guy with a can or two short of a six-pack but reliable and, once in a while, provided some good intel. Your report was really helpful; it gave us all the essential facts, but you also documented what you observed as well as what you didn't. Your notation about not finding a missing electrical cord just leapt off the page. We went through the entire house and didn't find a single missing cord. Which, of course, brought us to the question of where the cord came from.

"There's more. The cow tongue had a small, folded piece of paper with his name written on it. You probably saw the toothpicks used to keep it closed. In any case, it was written with a red marking pen. We couldn't find any red pen! On top of that, the piece of paper was torn from a larger page. We couldn't find that either, even though we had a team searching high and low.

"That tongue thing was a Brujaria, a Santeria spell. It's a warning or a spell not to talk. So, maybe he got so scared that he finished himself off, but it's looking more and more like someone came in and did the job. We're awaiting the tox screen, and we're still investigating."

"Amazing. Thanks for the update," I said.

"Jerry, keep up what you're doing, and you'll be every detective's friend. I'll let you know how it all pans out."

CHAPTER 77

The Crash

During my last week with Maria, I had an experience I'll never forget.

Maria and I were transporting to the station someone we had arrested for burglary. We were traveling on a road that crossed over a wide irrigation canal. As we approached the canal, we saw four or five cars parked on the side of the road, on the canal's overpass. Several people were running to the railing and looking over at something down below.

"We're not supposed to stop when transporting a prisoner," Maria said, "but we're stopping anyway to see what's going on. Jerry, go look. I'll stay with the car."

Maria pulled in behind the parked cars and hit the lights. I jumped out, and several people who had been looking over the railing ran up to me. A few of them were fiddling with their cell phones, apparently dialing 911. "Hurry!" one of them shouted. "Someone's down there!"

When I arrived at the spot where they had been gawking, I saw the reason for their panic. Down below, in the canal, on its side, was a large SUV. A woman was in the water, clinging to the half-submerged vehicle. She was shouting something, but I couldn't make out the words. I ran back to our patrol car and excitedly yelled to Maria, "There's a car and a woman in the water. Call Rescue. I'm going back down there."

Before Maria could respond, I turned around and ran toward the abutment. I was confronted by a six-foot chain-link fence, erected to keep people from climbing down under the overpass. Once I managed to scale the fence, with my eyes focused on the girl in the water, I started to make my way down the steep concrete embankment.

Then, to the right side of the embankment, I saw the body of a woman. She was clearly dead. Blood from her body was running down the abutment, and her limbs were splayed at odd angles; most of her clothes had been blown off by the force of the impact. I knew I couldn't do anything for her; I had to get the girl out of the water first.

When I got to the water's edge, I was about to rip off my gun belt and vest when I saw that she was moving fairly well. I stepped into the water and shouted, "Swim to me. Just look at me and swim. It's only a few feet. You can do it."

"I'm afraid."

"You can make it. It's not far. I'll come closer to you. Come on. Come on!"

"I can't."

"I'm right here. Give it a try."

After a long pause, she let go of the car and started swimming. I moved a bit farther into the canal to shorten the distance. She swam a few yards, and our fingertips almost touched. Then I grasped her hand—it was icy cold—and drew her to me. All the while, she was screaming, "My sister! My sister!" She seemed hysterical. I understood immediately what had happened; somehow the mangled woman must have been ejected from the SUV and was hurled into the abutment.

I pulled the girl onto the embankment and turned her away from where her sister lay. I then knelt in front of her, checking for injuries. All the while, she continued crying out, "My sister. My sister." I tried to reassure her that help for her sister was on the way; I said anything and everything I could think of to keep her from looking in her sister's direction. It seemed like hours before I heard sirens and saw the Fire-Rescue guys coming over the fence. I learned later that the response time was only nine minutes.

An EMT immediately took my place. I whispered, "Please keep her turned away from the body over there." The girl was slipping into shock and wasn't screaming anymore, just continuingly muttering, "My sister. My sister."

When other firemen came to the girl, I moved away from them and got on the radio. I advised dispatch that this was a traffic crash with a fatality and to start the highway patrol. Then I raised Maria and told her that I needed an emergency blanket, right away. She must have commandeered a civilian, because within a few minutes, a man appeared at the chain-link fence with a large yellow package. Without hesitation, he tossed it down to me.

I wanted to cover the woman's body quickly. Of course, I didn't want her sister to see it, but I didn't want her nearly naked body exposed to the eyes of all the rubberneckers. As I started to cover her up, I saw that she was about twenty and attractive.

I climbed up to the highway and walked back to our car. After explaining to Maria what I had done, she gave me an approving nod and said, "Jerry, start gathering witness information till the FHP (Florida Highway Patrol) gets here. I'll stay with the prisoner."

I was thankful for the assignment; it kept me busy and my thoughts away from the dead woman. As I interviewed several witnesses, a consistent story emerged: The SUV was traveling northbound when the driver swerved hard right to avoid a dog walking on the overpass. The driver seemed to lose control of the SUV, and it hit the guardrail at a speed and angle that sent it spilling over the rail into the canal. Several observers speculated that the passenger must not have had her seat belt on and was hurled out of the SUV'S open window or door, crashing into the embankment. The driver was fortunate that she wasn't trapped in the vehicle.

I was just finishing my witness interviews when the FHP car arrived. I turned over my notes to Trooper Jenkins, who seemed grateful for the work I had saved her.

When I got back to our car, I summarized what the witnesses had told me and about the woman's cries, "My sister. My sister."

Maria gently said, "Jerry, that was a bad scene. You did a good job; you did all that could be done. Now you need to get your head back into this game and your brain back into this police car."

"Sure," I replied, but the woman's plaintive cries weren't erasing easily.

Later, as we resumed patrol, Maria told me, "One lesson I learned long ago is to just hit the animal. It's a sad decision, but it's better than most other outcomes."

CHAPTER 78

Parting

It was the end of my last training day at the West Station. As I was emptying my locker, Maria said that she enjoyed working with me. She wished me happiness and success in the years ahead, and to my great surprise, she gave me a motherly hug.

It was a special moment for me. I felt affirmed and, yes, honored. I had a lot of respect for Maria and learned so much from her, especially about investigative techniques and report writing, all useful for my future.

And so, off I went to a new FTO and a new venture. For my third month of on-the-job training, I was transferred back to HQ Station. And, as expected, I was assigned to the midnight shift—1000 to 0600.

My new FTO was Tim Murphy, as Irish as the lakes of Killarney. He was a big man, rosy cheeked, with a large, rounded face and thinning grayish hair. Not quite handsome but close to it. He smiled a lot and seemed to be a happy guy. Tim was a bit paunchy; he reminded me of a slimmed down Santa Claus.

"Here's how we'll work," he explained as we walked to our patrol car. "We'll operate as though you were on your own—you'll drive, man the radio, and write the reports. I'll be your backup. If you have a question, ask. If you need help, let me know right away. Otherwise, consider these four weeks as a dress rehearsal for when you're by yourself. You okay with that?"

"Yes. That sounds perfect."

Unlike the day shifts I had just come off, things seemed relatively quiet during the night. On our first tour, we went for a few hours before we had our first call—a drunk walking down the beach, shouting obscenities at the ocean. When we approached him, he quickly calmed down and shamefacedly let us drive him home.

Tim and I had plenty of time to talk. I told him about Bridge's distaste for the midnight shift and asked him how he minded it.

"Well, Jerry, it's a long story, but since we seem to have plenty of free time, I'll tell you. We have two kids. My wife, Jo Ann, is a pediatric nurse; she works an eight-to-four shift at the hospital. I used to be a detective, but that involved being called out at all hours of the day and night; Jo Ann could never count on me to be available to help with the kids or anything. Sometimes I worked all night, and then, at nine in the morning, I had to be at court for four or five hours.

"We talked about it over and over, and we finally came to a decision. We decided it would be worth it if we took the financial hit and I switched back to being a uniform."

"You were a detective?"

"Yeah, that's right. Now I have regular hours, and I'm home during the day. We also have some evening time together. Not perfect, but right now, it works for us."

"What kind of detective?"

"I did economic crimes mostly."

"Like what?"

"Mail fraud, scams, stolen credit cards, phony checks, stuff like that. It's a lot of paperwork."

"At the academy, we had a lecture or two about economic crime; it seemed complicated."

"It is, but it is also very prevalent. Maybe we'll get a call on one before your month is up."

CHAPTER 79

Fraud

On our third week together, Tim's prediction came true; we received an economics crime call. It came at 2220, just as we were pulling out of the station.

"One-one-one-five. Signal twenty-four, possible fraud, 8124 Oleander Ave. Case number 341006."

"That's unusual," said Tim. "They typically are day or afternoon cases."

I replied, "HQ, one-one-one-five, ten-fifty-one to 8124 Oleander."

Five minutes later, I stopped the car a little to the right of the property, and we carefully looked around before we walked up to a well-lit, large, ranch-style house. The neighborhood was filled with similar well-kept homes.

We stood on opposite sides of the door. I knocked and announced, "Police!" An older woman, about sixty-five, opened the door. She was wearing a floor-length, colorful dress—quite nice, I thought, for so late in the evening. She invited us in and said, "I'm so embarrassed about this, but I spoke with my son on the phone tonight, and he told me to call the police, that I should report it as soon as possible."

"Okay," I said. "Tell us what the problem is, but first, what is your name?"

"Oh, of course. I'm Elena Mitchell."

I'm Officer Krone, and my partner is Officer Murphy."

The lady then directed us to a dining room table. At one end of the table, where she had apparently been sitting, were a few low stacks of paper. She invited us to have a seat, and then she explained that she had received a phone call about a month ago.

The man on the other end introduced himself and told her that he was an attorney who represented a lottery company and that she had won a lottery in Nova Scotia. Her name, he said, had been entered in the lottery because she had bought books online from a company based there.

Elena went on to say that the man seemed very nice and told her that she had won $250,000. But, since she was not a citizen, she would need, by Canadian law, to have an attorney represent her interest. The caller went on to say that the company that ran the lottery routinely retained him to handle these transactions two or three times a year.

"I was so excited," Elena said. "My grandson was just starting college, and I thought I would surprise him with a new car."

Then she told us the "attorney" explained that in order to collect her winnings, she would need to pay his retainer up front, as well as the Canadian tax on the winnings. The retainer, he said, was $1,000, and the tax was 7 percent. The lawyer told her she could get her money quite quickly if she provided the amounts as soon as possible. He further instructed her that she would need two cashier's checks or international money orders sent to a bank that he would name for her.

"Mrs. Mitchell, what was the total amount he wanted?" asked Tim.

"Call me, Elena, please. I'm sorry to say that the tax check would be for $17,500 and, of course, another $1,000 for the retainer."

Ouch, I thought.

Elena showed me a copy of an emailed letter announcing her prize. It stated that she would be contacted by an attorney to facilitate her collection of the winnings. It also specified the same information that the lawyer provided about the retainer and Canadian taxes.

I looked over at Tim and saw that he was furiously taking notes and also looking at all the documentation that Elena had laid out. His notes were neat and in columns.

Elena said that she had withdrawn the money from her bank in the form of two cashier's checks, addressed them as the instructions had dictated, and sent them off.

Almost in tears, she said, "All this occurred over a month ago, and since then, I've heard nothing. I tried to call the phone numbers on the email and the number I took down when talking to the lawyer, but there never was any answer."

"Were the checks cashed?" Tim asked.

"I called the bank, and they told me that both checks had been cashed. The money is gone," she mourned.

While I had taken a few notes, I was lost about what to do next.

I think Tim saw my uneasiness and kindly said, "Jerry, I got this. I've seen this scenario a number of times, so don't worry about the report. We'll write it up together."

He then faced the woman and said, "Elena, I'm so sorry, but the chances of your getting this money back are almost nil. In all likelihood, this money went to accounts in Nova Scotia and were then immediately wired out to banks in Nigeria or other centers for economic crime."

"So, that's it?" she said with obvious disappointment.

"Well," Tim replied, "we'll write a report for a detective in Investigations, and he'll contact you. He'll want to make copies of your check stubs, bank statements, emails, whatever other documentation you have here on the table or elsewhere. He'll also contact the FBI, but what they will do, I can't say."

Tearfully, Elena said, "And all I wanted to do was to surprise my grandson with a new car."

Tim tried to comfort her. "These people were very clever. You aren't the first one to be taken in. They usually prey on older folks who are more trusting, more used to a handshake society and not used to scams.

"Oh, another important point is that since they were successful in getting some money from you, they are likely to try again. This time it will be an entirely different scheme, so be on the alert. If anyone emails or calls and asks for information about you or for money, don't do anything except call your son or the police—right away."

"What has this world come to?" she lamented.

"Elena, would you like me to call your son and explain to him what I've told you?"

She seemed to like the idea, so Tim spoke with her son (John) and summarized all that he had told his mother, especially about being alert to future scams. Tim then handed the phone to Elena so she could talk with John. We silently waved goodbye and showed ourselves out.

As we drove away, I said to Tim, "That was a nice idea to speak with the son and then turn the phone over to Elena."

"I thought," he replied, "that if she were like other scam victims we've worked with, she was probably feeling alone and maybe violated. It was the best thing I could think to do."

"It was a great idea. I'll have to try to remember that."

"Now, Jerry, about the report. Let's go to Diane's coffee shop to work on it. Unlike our other calls, I think it will be most helpful if I write this one, and then we'll review it together."

"Sounds good."

As we sat in Diane's and Tim was busy writing, I could feel the rise of the same angry emotions I experienced some seven months ago when I left Nikki's house. Preying on elderly, innocent people like Elena wasn't right. I wanted to hunt them, stop them.

CHAPTER 80

Last Ride with Tim

The scam call stirred up my emotions and awakened the worried feelings I had about Nikki. In a few days, I'd be on my own and more able to look into the situation, so I thought it might be useful to discuss the case with Tim.

An opportunity to talk about Nikki occurred last night. It was about 0200; all of our reports were written, and the radio was silent. As we slowly cruised down Beach Road, I asked Tim if he remembered a call, around seven months ago, about a house being broken into and the victim's panties possibly being stolen.

"I haven't any recollection of it, Jerry. It doesn't sound like a big deal event."

"Well, it wasn't in the sense that anything of value was taken, maybe a panty, but it was very traumatic for the victim."

"Do you know her?"

"I didn't know her, but I was a trainee with Jose, on my first ride-along, when we caught the call. We were at her house twice, and I got to see firsthand how devastated she was. I want to get that guy."

"Hold it, Jerry. We have detectives who handle burglaries. Back off."

"I know that, but I'm going to track this guy down. I've got this case!"

"What do you mean, you've got this case?"

During the rest of the evening, I reviewed the whole case for Tim, including my run-ins with Detective DeSota and Goldy West, the detective sergeant.

"You were lucky to get out of that scrape. Next time, it may not work out for you."

"You think I should just give up on it? Not do anything?"

"No, I didn't mean that, Jerry. But you're going to have to proceed very carefully. As you have probably seen, DeSota has a big ego. Whatever you do, you'll have to take that into account and work within the system."

"I know what you mean about DeSota. You said I wouldn't have to give up on the case. Do you have any thoughts about how I can involve myself?"

"Yes, I do. First and foremost, keep DeSota informed. Don't surprise him. Explain that you'll be patrolling Nikki's part of town, that you'd be happy to be his eyes and feet on the ground, that you'll be his beat cop if he likes, and you'll be willing to follow up on any leads he'd like pursued. You can exploit his ego a bit by telling him it will free up his time for more important cases.

"And secondly, patrol the area as often as you can so you can learn what's normal and what's not. Be sure to document movements of people who look out of place or are up and about at unusual times.

"My third thought ties into documentation. Keep extensive notes. Every stop, every conversation, every observance. You can't gather too many facts. It's those facts that will convince your superiors that you're dedicated and serious about your work. It also will be your best defense against DeSota.

"Jerry, I wish you a lot of luck with this case. Just know that if ever I can be of help, call me. You have a good head on your shoulders; I'm sure you'll find your man. I've talked enough. Let's go get some coffee."

As Tim and I chatted on our break—talking a bit about my future—I felt some strange, uneasy vibes. They probably stemmed from the fact that I was coming to the end of my three months of on-the-job training; in a few days, I would be cut loose. It wasn't that I was afraid to go out on my own but more, I think, that I was leaving three FTOs that I had grown to admire and respect.

Some people might label my uneasy feelings as "transition blues." But that wouldn't be accurate. I wasn't feeling blue at all; instead, I felt upbeat. For one thing, I lucked out on my shift assignment. Most rookies start off on the graveyard shift, but last week at roll call, the sergeant announced that I'd be starting on afternoons. But, of course, the main reason for my ebullience was that I was finally going to be a cop on my own.

CHAPTER 81

Solo Ride

I was elated, much like I felt after passing my driver's license test, especially when Mom said, "Okay, Jerry, drive us home." It was finally going to happen; after nine months of training, I was going to fly solo. I was going to have my own patrol car.

While driving to the station, my mind kept calling up images—like film clips—of calls that I had experienced during my training. I wondered what scenes I would encounter today.

As I approached HQ, my cell phone rang. It was Bridge. My face lit up as I switched to Bluetooth.

"Hi, big shot. How's it going? How are you feeling about going off by yourself for the first time?"

"Bridge, I'm excited. I feel energized and alive."

"Wonderful! I wanted you to know that I'll be praying for a safe shift."

"Thanks. I'll let you know how it went. Probably I'll hit the sack when I get home, but I'll call you about noon or as soon as I wake up."

"Great. I can't wait to hear about your tour. I love you."

"I love you too. I'm so happy that you called. It's always nice to hear your voice."

At the roll call, Sergeant Wilson gave the unit assignments for the four cars that were going out on the two-to-ten shift. Mine was the last one mentioned. "And for Officer Krone, unit one-three-one-seven." With that, he tossed me the keys and said, "Stay safe out there."

I knew, as a rookie, that I'd be getting the oldest, most beat-up vehicle in the lot. But I didn't care. It was mine, and I was beginning a career that felt just right for me.

I picked up my backpack and the shotguns and made my way out to the parking lot. In north Florida during October, the climate was usually hot and humid, but that afternoon seemed to be the exception. The humidity was low, the temperature a balmy seventy-five with no rain in the forecast.

As expected, the car keys were not for an up-to-date SUV that most officers were driving but instead an old Crown Vic. It was dinged here and there, smelly inside, and a candidate for replacement. I stowed the guns, turned on the computer and radio, adjusted my seat belt, and turned the key. To my surprise, the 350-horsepower engine immediately fired up, sounding smooth and powerful.

Leaving the gate, I radioed dispatch: "One-three-one-seven, ten-eight."

"One-three-one-seven, ten-four."

As soon as the dispatcher said, "ten-four," my radio produced numerous click sounds, like the sound that's made whenever you engage your microphone. I had heard about this practice at the academy but forgotten about it. It's a way that others on duty say, "Welcome aboard."

The clicks brought a smile to my face. I thought there probably weren't many other jobs where you get so warmly welcomed. I felt proud knowing that now I was seen as one of them.

An entire afternoon and early evening lay ahead of me. This was a heady moment. I was in charge, and I could drive wherever I wanted in zone one. I felt almost giddy. One place I was planning to visit was Seabrook Avenue and Nikki's neighborhood. But I thought I'd first cover a location that the sergeant mentioned during roll call— Fairmount Elementary School. Several calls from parents had complained about cars speeding in the school zone.

I was parked on a side street near the school when the radio blared. It had been so quiet it startled me.

"One-three-one-seven, signal eighty-two, found wallet, 2811 Palmetto Avenue, a Mrs. Rice. Case 341645."

"One-three-one-seven, ten-four, ten-fifty-one to 2811 Palmetto."

When I arrived at 2811, I thought about the countless times my FTOs told me not to pull up in front of a destination house. So, I parked at the right-hand side of the property. The house looked new. It was two stories, with white siding and black shutters. The shrubbery surrounding the house was mostly young plants that were still low to the ground. A white Toyota Highlander was parked in the driveway.

A young, dark-haired woman, trim, maybe late twenties, answered the door. She wore very brief red running shorts and a gray sports bra. Sexy. It looked as though she was ready to head out for a run.

"Oh, hello, Officer, thank you for coming so quickly." Seemingly a little embarrassed, she glanced down at her outfit and continued, "I was wondering how long I'd have to wait before I could go for my run. Just a minute, and I'll get the wallet."

She returned in less than a minute and handed it to me. It was red and yellow plaid and quite thin. A zipper opened and closed it like a small purse. Years ago, my mother had one that was quite similar, so I concluded that it belonged to a woman.

"I found it about ten minutes ago in the Publix parking lot, the one over on Tenth Avenue."

I opened the wallet and in a clear plastic sleeve saw a driver's license. The wallet belonged to Jeanne Ostler of 84 Lakeland Avenue, apartment 3B. The picture on her license showed her to be blonde with an attractive face. She was twenty-eight. The wallet contained eighteen dollars, two credit cards, and a variety of stubs. I gave Mrs. Rice a receipt for the wallet and the eighteen dollars and thanked her for calling us and for being a good citizen. I also asked if I could give Ms. Ostler her name and address, should she ask; she agreed.

I wasn't very familiar with Ms. Ostler's part of town, so I used the GPS to guide me to Lakeland; it took only fifteen minutes. Eighty-four Lakeland turned out to be a redbrick, four-story apartment building. Nothing fancy. I rang the button for 3B, and it was answered by a woman who sounded rushed and impatient.

"Who is it?"

"The police. Are you Jeanne Ostler?"

"No, she isn't here. I heard she moved out last year. Why do you want her?"

"Do you know where she moved to?"

"No, I never met her. I haven't any idea where she went. Why are you asking about her?"

"Thanks for your help, ma'am," I replied and then quickly released the intercom button.

I returned to my car and looked through the wallet for anything that might help me find her. And there it was, a check stub from Atlantic Coast Sails. It was possible, I thought, that it was from a payroll check, so I went on the computer and brought up their website. They were sailmakers on, would you believe it, Atlantic Avenue. I knew that street; it was just a few blocks from several large marinas.

CHAPTER 82

The Upside

Atlantic Coast Sails was housed in a low, warehouse-type building with a small, glass-enclosed showroom facing the street. Five or six parking spaces separated the curb and the building. Inside, hoisted on miniature masts, were displays of sails of different shapes and fabrics.

Two men working at a large, flat table seemed to be examining naval engineering drawings.

"Yes, Officer, can we help you?"

"Yes, do you have an employee by the name of Jeanne Ostler?"

"Yes, Jeanne works here part-time. Is there a problem?"

"Oh, no," I replied. "Someone found her wallet, and I'm trying to track her down so we can return it."

"Just a minute."

He returned with a page from a notepad on which he had written Jeanne's address. "Would you like me to call her to see if she's home?"

"That would be great. Thanks."

He made the call, but there was no answer. He gave me the sheet with Ms. Ostler's address; I thanked them for their help and left.

With no calls from dispatch, I decided that I might as well go to the address the sailmaker had given me and see if I could find the wallet's owner. I was enjoying this investigating.

Jeanne's address was on Turtle Creek Drive. It was located in an older neighborhood. The houses looked like early Florida—stucco cottages with front porches and tile roofs well set back from the road. Sprawling oaks and palm trees dominated the landscape. Here and there, a few houses looked shabby, but for the most part, it looked like a nice, quiet neighborhood.

As I stepped onto the porch, I could hear the sound of a TV. I rang the bell and waited almost a minute before the door opened. In the doorway, a young woman saw me and, clearly startled, exclaimed, "Oh, my God, what's the matter?"

"Nothing, ma'am," I quickly said. "I have something for Jeanne Ostler."

"That's me."

"I tried to reach you by phone just a few minutes ago, but there was no answer."

"I didn't hear the phone ring. My mother is hard of hearing, and she keeps the TV on really loud. What's this all about?"

"Are you missing your wallet?"

"No, Officer, I don't think so. It's in my pocketbook."

"Would you mind looking for it?"

She returned, looking puzzled and anxious. Her pocketbook was wide open, and she was furiously rummaging through it. "I can't believe it's not here. I can't believe it's not here," she repeated.

No wonder she had never phoned in; she never realized that her wallet was gone. "I have some good news," I said with a smile. "I have your wallet. Can you describe it for me?"

"Well, sure. It's made of cloth, a red and yellow plaid. It has a zipper around it."

"Is this it?"

"Oh, thank you, thank you." Her eyes teared.

"There was eighteen dollars in it. Is that about what you had?"

"Yeah, that's probably right. I had just finished shopping, and that's what was left. Where was it found?"

"In the Publix parking lot, the one on Tenth Avenue."

"It must have slipped out of my hands as I was loading the car. I'd like to thank whoever it was that retrieved it. Are you allowed to tell me their name?"

"Yes, she gave me permission. Her name is Mrs. Rice, and her number is right here. I've jotted it down on your receipt for the wallet."

"Oh, thank you."

"Ms. Ostler, there's one other thing. Your driver's license

has not been updated since you moved from the apartment on Lakeland Avenue. You should take care of it right away."

"I will. I'll do it first thing tomorrow."

As I walked back to the patrol car, I felt great. So many of my patrols involved tragedy or sadness, and here was one that ended joyfully. What a nice way to begin my solo tour.

CHAPTER 83

Belligerence

The euphoric feeling from returning the wallet didn't last long. Within ten minutes, I heard the dispatcher call, "One-three-one-four" (another car out on patrol).

"One-three-one-four."

"One-three-one-four, vehicle on Eighth and Maple, red pickup, complaints about loud music."

"Ten-four. Ten-fifty-one to Eighth and Maple."

The address was not far from the airport and only a mile or so from where I was patrolling. It was in an area known for drug activity and violent crime. I radioed that I would respond as a backup, an expected action if you were not on call.

As I pulled up to the scene, the officer with the call—Cynthia Martell, a woman I recognized from being with her during many roll calls—was standing next to a huge man. He was built like a linebacker. It was clear from the snarl on his face and his clenched fists that he was going to be confrontational. I got out of the car, and when I was about twenty feet away, I heard Cynthia shout, "I need to see your driver's license."

"I don't got to show you shit," he blustered, kicking off his sandals at the same time.

Cynthia, trying to be patient, said, "You got a license?"

"Fuck you," the man replied and pulled off his T-shirt.

I knew from talking with other officers that this was how streetwise subjects prepared to fight. They had learned that sandals impaired their mobility, and the absence of a shirt made it difficult for opponents to grapple or hold on.

Cynthia asked again to see his license and got no response other than a defiant stare. Instinct told me it was time to act, so I moved in and grabbed the man's right arm in an attempt to control him before he swung at either of us. As I tried to lever his right arm behind his back and get him to the ground, he pulled his sweaty arm away. All I could do was get him in a headlock. I had lost track of what Cynthia was doing. The fight was on.

As I tried once more to get him to the ground in a headlock, he turned his head and bit down hard on my left bicep. A sharp pain jolted me. I screamed and let go. The man turned and raced toward a low chain-link fence, vaulted it, and ran off. I saw Cynthia chasing him, and I started to follow but noticed blood streaming down my arm; I was bleeding heavily. I got on the radio and screamed, "One-three-one-seven, signal thirty-four, one-three-one-seven, ten-thirty-four, code three!"

I radioed our location, described the man, and stated that he was running in a northbound direction. I wanted to recommend perimeter locations, but not being familiar with all the local streets, I said, "Make the perimeter three blocks north and three blocks on the east and west sides. Have another unit call it."

I sank to the ground next to my car, breathing hard from my brief fight. I continued with my radio transmission, advising that I had been injured.

At that moment, the air was filled with the sounds of sirens; my sergeant, Dan Lynne, along with several other patrol cars, screeched to a stop next to my car. The sarge looked down at my arm and saw the silver-dollar-sized hole on the inside of my bicep. Instantly, he called to one of the arriving officers and yelled, "Randy, get your first aid kit."

He then faced me and said, "Relax, Jerry. We've got this."

I watched as Sergeant Lynne began radioing adjustments to the perimeter and calling for a helicopter and a K-9 unit.

Randy returned with his kit and gazed down at my wound and my name tag. "Hey, Krone," he said, "let's get this cleaned up and covered. This is going to hurt; human bites are bad."

He sprayed foam alcohol all over the wound and then dressed it with a cloth bandage tied around my arm. I could hear all the radio traffic, but it seemed like it was all mumbling. Then Sarge told Randy, "Get him to the hospital."

I got into Randy's car, and off we went, code three. About fifteen minutes later, we arrived at Mercy Hospital. Randy got me into the emergency room, sought out the charge nurse, and spoke to her. There were about six to eight people in the ER, but the nurse took one look at the bloody bandage and said, "Let's go!"

She handed me off to another nurse, who said she'd take care of me. She asked about what had happened, and as I described the incident, she undressed the wound and winced when she saw it. She looked at me and said, "I'll do some cleaning up here, and a doctor will come in. You'll need some sutures, but you'll be okay. Get ready now. This is going to hurt some."

As she cleaned out the wound, it did hurt like hell. She tried chatting in an attempt to distract me, but it wasn't working. All the while, they were administering antibiotic IVs, hoping to halt a possible HIV infection. I was also given a tetanus shot.

After the doctor completed the stitches, we had to wait for an hour or so for the IV to empty. Then Randy drove me back to the station where the sarge informed me that a K-9 officer caught the guy about two blocks away, inside the perimeter I had set up. "Funny," he said. "The perp wasn't interested in fighting a dog; he gave up right away. You did a good job, Jerry. Now go home. The detectives have this now; they'll be in touch. Call me tomorrow."

Sarge asked if I needed a ride, and if so, he would have someone follow with my car. I thanked him and said I thought I'd be okay, but I'd need a ride to the scene to retrieve my car. I was still in pain but didn't comment about it.

On the drive home, I thought about something that Jose, my first ride-along FTO, had told me. He said, "Jerry, the job isn't all doughnuts and coffee." He was so right. As a cop, I'd experienced a lot of satisfaction, but there were also many tragedies and sad events. And now the physical hurt. I was quite aware that there was a risk in being a cop, but thus far, the ups far outweighed the downs.

I wondered how long Sarge would keep me off active duty.

CHAPTER 84

Reactions

Driving down Cardinal Lane, I began anticipating my mother's reaction to me arriving home early. I was dreading pulling into our driveway. I was certain, too, it would get worse once she spotted my bandaged arm; it would really hit the fan.

I tried to prepare myself for the onslaught, but for the moment, I couldn't come up with an appeasing explanation. I knew I'd have to take it, as they say, like a man.

The minute I walked through the doorway, Mom screamed, "My God, what happened to you?"

"Oh, it's nothing, Mom. I'm really okay."

"You're home early from work, and you walk in here with that big bandage on your arm; don't tell me it's nothing."

"It's a minor thing, Mom. I got hurt trying to arrest a man."

"That's exactly what I was afraid of when you joined the force. Being a cop is a dangerous thing."

"Mom, whenever there is an injury, the sergeant takes you off duty and sends you home. It's standard procedure. I'm going to be just fine."

"You're sure?"

"Yes, Mom, I'm sure."

"Well, what exactly happened to your arm?"

"A man I was arresting bit it, but it's just a scratch. It's nothing to worry about."

"That sounds terrible, but I'm so glad it's not serious. I can't imagine anybody doing that. Look, I was about to brew a cup of tea. Would you like some?"

"Sounds perfect. Let's relax. I'll go change out of my uniform. Everything's okay."

But, of course, everything wasn't perfect. My arm hurt like hell.

After a while, I said, "Mom, they told me to take it easy, so I'm going upstairs to stretch out a bit."

"That's a good idea, Jerry. Your body has had a trauma; it's calling for rest."

Sometime later, I was awakened by a knock on my bedroom door. Then I heard, "Jerry. It's Dad. Are you okay?"

He came in, sat on the bed, and calmly asked, "What happened?"

I told him the entire story from my arrival at the scene to my drive home.

"So, how badly are you hurt?"

"It was a nasty bite and took about six stitches; however, I didn't tell Mom about that part. But, Dad, the stitches weren't the worst of it. It's my pride; the guy got the best of me."

"Jerry, you can't win every time. There is always going to be someone bigger, or stronger, or tougher. That's a reality in life. Tell me, did you learn anything from it?"

"Well, maybe I should have acted sooner and moved in before he was fully ready to attack. But, Dad, the real lesson is that I should have immediately called for backup. It wasn't smart to take on this guy by myself."

"You're right. You're still very young, Jerry, but you're not invincible. When you pick a fight—"

"Thanks, Dad," I interrupted. "I learned a lot from this call."

I decided to take a couple of Tylenol and then give Bridge a call.

CHAPTER 85

Beach Walk

I wasn't at all certain how Bridge would react to my injury. Would she see it simply as part of a cop's job, or would she see it as a significant issue—something that might get in the way of us as a couple? I knew we had to talk.

We were going out on Saturday night, but I couldn't wait until then. I decided to call.

"Hey, Bridge. I'd like to talk with you about something. How about going for a walk on the beach, maybe after dinner?"

"Oh, that sounds serious. What do you want to discuss?"

"Nothing critical. I just want to get together. Suppose I pick you up at seven?"

"Okay. See you then."

I decided not to shock her with my large bandage, so I wore a light nylon jacket. It was a beautiful night. The sea breeze had slackened so that the ocean was calm; small, one-foot waves gently splashed on the beach. I couldn't have asked for a more pleasant setting.

As we strolled along, Bridge asked, "What was it you wanted to talk about?"

Since Bridge had some experience at being a cop, I relayed to her the whole story, much like I had told Dad. She expressed, appropriately, her shock at the news and her sorrow for my injury. Then she said, "Jerry, it's odd. The on-the-job dangers didn't trouble me when I was on duty, but now they worry me terribly. It reminds me of the phrases you often hear, 'When a cop leaves for work, you never know if he's coming back.'"

"Are you trying to say something about us?"

"I don't know, Jerry. I'm just thinking out loud. I guess that being off the job changes your perceptions some. But hey, let's not overreact. I knew you were a cop when I agreed to our commitment to each other, but, being completely honest with you, I worry when you're out there on patrol."

"I'm sorry you have that burden."

"Well, it's just a fact of life. Jerry, relax. My worry is not going to stop me from wanting to be with you."

"Thank you for saying that, Bridge. I love you and want you to be part of my life. I can't promise you I won't take any chances, but I will promise to act smarter."

"Okay, I'll accept that. Give me a kiss and let's enjoy the rest of our walk."

"Just don't squeeze my left arm."

Later that night, I sensed that we had hurtled a likely future obstacle. Maybe it would still be an issue from time to time, but I saw our discussion as a growth step. For now, so far, so good.

CHAPTER 86

Sarge's Announcement

By the beginning of my second solo week, my arm was fully healed. On that same afternoon, a roll call announcement got my juices flowing. Among six or seven other items, Sarge said, "Last night, there was a call reference from a Mrs. Dawson about a prowler walking through her backyard at 7842 Williamson Street. The suspect was unidentified but thought to be male. Keep an eye out."

Williamson Street. Where did I hear that before? I sat for a few minutes in the patrol car and looked up Williamson Street. It only took a second for me to realize why it sounded familiar. It turned out that Williamson was the road that intersected Seabrook, one block away from Nikki's house. At once, I knew where I was going to spend a lot of patrolling time.

Unfortunately, my visit to Nikki's neighborhood was delayed by a string of calls that needed my response—two fender benders and a missing pet. It wasn't until near five o'clock that I was able to check out Seabrook and the nearby streets.

I decided to drive past Nikki's, and as I approached her house, I saw a white Camry pulling into her driveway. I remembered that Nikki drove one just like it. Amazed at my good fortune, I parked on the street at the end of her driveway, got out of the car just as Nikki was exiting hers, and shouted, "Hi, Nikki!"

Nikki turned and was a bit startled at seeing a uniform in her driveway. "It's Jerry Krone."

Nikki looked puzzled at first, but then she must have recognized me and, with a smile, waved and called, "Hi, Jerry. What's up?"

We stood chatting in the driveway until I thought an appropriate amount of time had passed for me to ask, "Is there anything new with the case?"

She answered by telling me that once the new locks and alarm system were installed, and after I repaired the fence, everything had been quiet. She also said that she hadn't heard from the detective recently, so she didn't know if anyone had been arrested or not. She said that she assumed the case was on the back burner. I told her that if an arrest had been made, the detective would have contacted her.

I explained that I was now assigned to that part of town and I'd be patrolling the area as much as I could. But, for fear of raising her anxiety, I decided, for now, not to tell her about the prowler.

Nikki invited me in, but I told her that I had to continue my patrol. She extended her hand for a shake, and then each of us, in our own way, indicated that we hoped we would see each other soon.

As I drove away, I pondered about how much to say, if anything, to Detective DeSota about my visit with Nikki. I didn't want him to think that I was reopening his case, but I couldn't think of a better way to handle the situation except to talk with him, something I definitely wasn't looking forward to.

CHAPTER 87

DeSota

I decided to bite the bullet and talk with DeSota. It was an action that Tim, my FTO, had suggested, and I hadn't come up with a better alternative. I figured that, at the least, he'd know I was patrolling in Nikki's neighborhood and that I wasn't going behind his back.

I came in early for my 1400 start and went upstairs to the detective tables. And, lucky me, DeSota was at his desk, talking on his phone. So many file folders littered the desk that I could hardly see its surface. He saw me approach and raised his hand in the air with a finger extended. I took the gesture to mean, "Wait a minute, and I'll be with you."

When the detective hung up, he said in an irritated voice, "Hey, Krone, what are you doing up here?"

"Have you got a minute?" I asked.

"No, I don't have a minute. As you can see, I'm up the kazoo with cases, but I'll make a minute. What's on your mind?"

"Well, as you can see, I'm now on the road, and I'm assigned the patrol area that includes Nikki Wilson's house. I wanted to bring you up to date on something."

"What?" he impatiently growled.

"I want you to know that I'm following up on a reported prowler near Seabrook, in Mrs. Wilson's neighborhood. I didn't want you to think that I'm in any way interfering with your case—"

"Good thing," he interrupted.

"But since I'm going to be in the area, I'd be happy to pursue any leads you'd like checked out. I could be your eyes and legs on the ground."

"Thanks, kid. I appreciate your keeping me informed. That's important. And if I need something checked out, I'll contact you. Otherwise, just keep your eyes and ears open."

"One other thing," I quickly threw out. "While patrolling the neighborhood yesterday, I saw Nikki Wilson pulling into her driveway, so I stopped to say hello. I didn't want you to hear about that from someone else."

"What the fuck are you doing? You were told to stay away from the case."

"It was just a social visit."

"Don't give me that shit. Don't mess where you don't belong."

Things were going downhill fast. I thought this conversation might have been a bridge builder, but now our relationship was probably worse than before. It seemed that whatever I said triggered a negative reaction. I felt angry and frustrated, much like the time, many years ago in the fifth grade, when I swung at Buzz. But I kept my cool and didn't swing. I thought, *How sad. The guy is obviously busy but has too big an ego to say something like, "Any info would be welcome."*

"I'm not messing in your case. I was just trying to be helpful. Too bad you can't see that."

With that comment, I turned away from him and left. Back downstairs, I took a few minutes to get my notes up to date, just as Tim had suggested.

When roll call was over, I went to my sergeant's office, Sarge Jordon, and described to him what had just happened upstairs with DeSota. I also gave him a synopsis of the confrontation (about Nikki's case) that I had with DeSota when I was still at the academy.

"Everyone who has worked with him knows he's a hothead," the sarge said. "Your experience isn't unique. You did the right thing, Jerry. One way our uniform patrol can be helpful to detectives is by gathering information or following up on things needing to be checked out. Too bad his ego gets in the way of your helping him."

CHAPTER 88

The Bike

As I was leaving the station, I decided to patrol the Williamson Street area twice a day—once in the afternoon and then between eight and ten at night. I thought that the evening patrolling was essential because that was when the prowler had been spotted.

At around 1500, on my first pass through the neighborhood, all was peaceful. I didn't see anyone out walking, much less a prowler. But about 2100, I had a very different experience.

I was cruising slowly along Sandhill Avenue and came upon a kid on his bike. I didn't think much about it, except that the red taillight, mounted on the back of the seat, was unlit. I stopped the car alongside of him, rolled down the passenger-side window, and said, "Hold it a minute. I want to talk with you."

The cyclist laid his bike against the curb, and I got out of the car. He was a young teenager, thin, not very tall, maybe five three, with ragged, sandy-colored hair. He had a pleasant-looking face, but it was marred by a few acne eruptions. He was wearing dark jeans, a black T-shirt, and a dark Jaguar's hat. He seemed tense.

"Is something wrong, Officer?"

"No, nothing serious, but I noticed that your taillight is not lit; you should have it on when riding at night."

"Oh," the boy said. "It's broken."

"Even so, try to turn it on; let's see if it works."

The teenager flipped the switch on the lamp, and it immediately lit up; I was surprised that he wasn't surprised.

I grabbed my warning-notice pad from the door pocket, got out of the car, and walked up to him and his bike. "What is your name?" I asked.

"Tyler."

"What's your full name, Tyler?"

"Tyler Clifford."

"How old are you?"

"Fifteen."

"Okay, Tyler, it's against the law to ride at night without your lights on; you should also be wearing your helmet. This time, I'm not going to give you a ticket; I'm going to write you a warning. But if it happens again, you'll be ticketed. Do you understand?"

"Oh, yes I do. Thank you so much for the warning; I won't forget it again."

"Good. Now tell me, what's your address and birthdate?"

I wrote out the warning notice, and as I handed it to Tyler, I asked, "Where were you going this time of night?"

"Oh, I was coming home from a basketball game at Fairmount Junior High. My friend's brother plays on the team, so I went to watch for a while."

"I see," I said. "Well, wear your helmet, keep your lights on, and ride safely."

As I drove away from Tyler, my brain wasn't at peace. Something kept tugging at it, drawing me back to my encounter with Tyler. What was it? *Well*, I thought, *one was his last name, Clifford. Why did that sound familiar?* I knew I had heard it before, but I couldn't place where. Something to do with another case?

The second item was Tyler's taillight not being turned on even though it was working perfectly well. His headlight was on; why turn on one light and not both? I argued with myself that people often forget such things, but when I pointed out to him that his taillight was off, he didn't seem to be the least bit surprised. Did he purposely keep it off?

I decided to drive past Tyler's house. It was on Palm Meadow, a street I was going to patrol anyway, but beyond that, I hoped that it might resolve some of the issues I was puzzling over.

Tyler's home, at 481 Palm Meadow, was two stories, unlike the many one-floor ranch-style homes built when that section of town was being developed. Suddenly, it struck me that Nikki's street, Seabrook, was the next block over, and that her house number was also 481! *Wait a minute*, I thought. *What's this?*

CHAPTER 89

Sarge's Advice

I thought I knew the answer, but I needed to check it out. I drove down Palm Meadow to the next cross street, Orchid Avenue, turned right and proceeded a short distance down Orchid, to Seabrook, turned onto Seabrook, and stopped in front of 481. Since Nikki's home was a single-level ranch, I could easily see over her roof to Tyler's two-story home on Palm Meadow. As I suspected, the houses were back-to-back.

I banged my fist on the steering wheel, over and over again. I couldn't believe what I had discovered—Tyler could possibly look down from his second floor and see into the Wilson house.

As I drove back to the station, my mind continued swirling. Should I tell anyone about my findings, or should I investigate further? *After all*, I thought, *all that I have for now is the fact that Tyler lives in a house directly behind Nikki's.*

Like scratching an itch, I couldn't stop my mind from trying to put the pieces together. Tyler was thin, of slight build. He could easily have slipped through what used to be the opening in Nikki's fence. But why would he break in?

Why did he open her panty drawer? Of course, Tyler was a young teenager. Maybe he was just curious about woman's underthings, or it could be something compulsive, like a fetish. A shrink would know.

Well, one thing I knew for sure—I was going to talk with Tyler again. I also thought it would be helpful if I could discuss this whole situation with somebody else.

Once back at the station, I decided to tell Sarge about my encounter with Tyler. I told him about the bike stop, the warning, and the discovery of Tyler's proximity to Nikki's. He listened without interrupting and then said, "Jerry, you're treading on dangerous ground here. If DeSota gets wind of this, he'll make trouble for you. At this point, we don't know if Tyler had anything to do with Nikki, but it sounds to me that he's a prime suspect for your prowler. Why don't you proceed to establish whether or not Tyler's the prowler—an investigation we can clearly justify. Jerry, remember, good investigations are objective; you let the leads dictate the direction. No one can then question your methods."

"Thanks, Sarge. That makes sense to me. You know, I first heard about the prowler at roll call this morning. Have there been any other sightings like that?"

"Come to think of it, I do recall something similar. It was several months ago, when you were still at the academy. Hold on for a minute; let me look it up."

The sarge went to his computer, and after several key punches, he said, "Ah, here it is. This incident occurred during the middle of the day, not at night. A woman reported that a young boy came into her backyard and stole panties off her clothesline. She yelled at him, and he ran off."

"He stole some panties? That sounds like the Nikki case."

"Do you have her address?"

"Sure, here's what we have."

He printed out the one-page sheet and handed it to me. It had the summary of her call along with her name, address, and telephone number. I noted that her address was 2643 Westwood Avenue.

"Westwood Avenue. Where's that, Sarge?"

"Oh, it's one of those streets next to Central Park."

Interesting, I thought. *That's not far from Palm Meadow and Tyler's house.* "Thanks, Sarge," I said. "I've got some investigating to do."

"Whoa," Sarge interrupted. "Just wait a minute. This is back to panties and most likely the Nikki case. Stay away from it, Jerry; for now, stick with the prowler call. That's an order."

CHAPTER 90

Yearbooks

It was around 1500 hours when I pulled into the parking lot behind Fairmount School. The building was a low, sprawling structure, shaped like a rectangle, with a large, parklike courtyard in the center. It reminded me of the Pentagon but with only four sides. It served as the junior high for the entire town, with classes for grades six to nine.

I had called ahead and was told that a guard would meet me at the Fairmount Avenue entrance. When I exited my car, I saw a sign, "Administrative Offices," and as I headed toward it, a gray-haired man looked out at me through a large window in the entry door.

As I neared the door, it opened, and I was met with a warm "Good afternoon, Officer." Then, pointing with his arm, he said, "The office you want is in that first door on the right."

I was still amazed how the uniform and badge commanded respect and made access easier, at least in some situations.

When I entered the office, I was greeted by an attractive young woman who was seated at a computer. I thought that she couldn't have been much older than eighteen. At once, my eyes were drawn to her long hair. It was a beautiful color with strands having an appealing blend of red and blonde. The sight was striking and easy on the eye.

"Can I help you?" she asked.

"Yes," I said with a smile. "I have two questions. First, last night, was there a junior high basketball game here at the gym?"

"No, there was nothing going on in the school last night. In fact, all of our junior high basketball games are played in the afternoon; it's the high school that often plays at night, but they play at the high school."

"Okay, thanks. My second question is, Do you have copies here of the school's yearbooks?"

"I'm not sure, but there might be copies in the library. It's just down the hall; I'll show you the way and introduce you to the librarian."

The library was a pleasant room with windows all along the far wall. The librarian, Mrs. Marshall, a middle-aged, overweight woman, seemed annoyed at our intrusion into her quiet domain. When I asked about the yearbooks, she told me, "We don't keep yearbooks here anymore. Too many of them disappeared."

"Well, does somebody in the school have them?" I asked.

"What are you looking for?" she challenged.

"I'm sorry, Mrs. Marshall; that's confidential right now."

Reluctantly, she indicated that Mrs. Cavanaugh, the school activities director, might have them. With that, she picked up her desk phone, hit an extension button, and spoke with the AD. In an unexpected act of helpfulness, she offered to retrieve the books.

"What years are you interested in?" she asked.

I told her the last three graduations, and off she went. When she returned with the books and handed them to me, she cautioned in a condescending tone, "When you're finished, don't leave them on the table; bring them directly to me." I got the not-so-subtle message: she made me feel like a seventh grader.

The library was empty, so I thanked Mrs. Marshall and took the yearbooks to a table that was out of her sight. I started with last year's book and quickly leafed through the pages until I got to the Cs. And there it was, along with eight other students—some male, some female—a head and shoulders yearbook photo of Tyler Clifford. He looked just about the same as when we met a few nights ago.

I asked Mrs. Marshall about using the library's copy machine, and she pointed it out to me. I made two copies of Tyler's yearbook page and then dutifully returned the three yearbooks to the librarian. As I put them down on her desk, she asked, "Did you find what you wanted?"

"Yes, I did. And thank you again for locating the yearbooks, but now I need one more bit of help. Do you have a black marking pen I can borrow?"

"As a matter of fact, I do," she said, reaching into her left-hand desk drawer.

I used the pen to black out all the names listed below each of the nine photos, so that only heads and shoulders were seen but no names. And, before the nosey Mrs. Marshall could ask another question, I returned the marking pen, thanked her, and rapidly left the library.

Once I got into my car, I couldn't let go of the fact that Tyler had lied to me.

CHAPTER 91

Mrs. Dawson

The house at 7842 Williamson Street turned out to be in a neighborhood like many in Florida. The houses were built by a single developer with a basic model, but each house was slightly unique because the builder varied the roof line, or dormer, or paint color. They were all two-story, two-car garage structures, placed on the smallest lots that zoning allowed.

The doorbell was answered by a stout, middle-aged woman; she was carrying a small cat in her arms.

"Oh, hello, Officer. What can I do for you?"

"I'm Officer Krone. Are you Mrs. Dawson?"

"Yes."

"Well, I'm following up on your phone call yesterday about the person you saw in your yard."

"I'm so glad you're here. It was quite upsetting."

"Tell me what you saw."

"Well, I was going around the house, checking the doors, you know, making sure they were locked, and when I got to the back door, I opened it to look out and check the weather. And there, between my house and the Hesses', was this kid. He was near the sidewalk but still in our yards. I think he saw me in the lighted doorway, and then he quickly went to the sidewalk and walked, sort of ran, down Williamson Street."

"You said *he*. How did you know he was a he?"

"I don't know. He just struck me as being a boy. His hair wasn't very long, he was dressed like a boy, and I'd say he ran like a boy."

"Do you remember what he was wearing?"

"Again, I'm not sure; there wasn't much light. But all his clothing was dark—dark shirt and pants and oh, yes, a baseball hat. When he looked in my direction, I could see from the street lamp an emblem on the cap; it was a light color, maybe yellow, and looked like the head of a tiger."

I could hardly contain my excitement. That "yellow tiger" described the Jaguar's symbol. It was on all their NFL merchandise; it was exactly like the one on Tyler's hat! I decided to see what else I could learn.

"That's very helpful, Mrs. Dawson. How about his size. Tall? Short? What?"

"Oh, that's easy. He definitely was thin—a slight build. Not at all tall. He struck me as being young, maybe thirteen or fourteen."

I pulled my notebook from my back pocket and retrieved from it the yearbook page I had copied and blackened. I showed it to Mrs. Dawson and asked, "Is boy you saw in any one of these photos?"

She studied the pictures for about thirty seconds and said, "He had a thin face, like a couple of these, but it was really too dark to make out any features. I'm sorry."

"No problem. You've been very helpful. Anything else you can think of?"

"No, I can't think of anything else. I'm surprised that I remembered so much."

"I appreciate your time and help. A detective may also want to talk with you, but in the meantime, let's hope we find the boy."

I drove to Oak Park, a quiet place that Jose, my first FTO, showed me. It was about six o'clock, dinnertime for many, so the streets were relatively empty. It was a perfect time for me to consolidate my notes—to get them organized for when I had to write the report about all I had been doing. I also hoped there would be a pause in radio calls; I wanted some time to plan how I was going to proceed with Tyler.

CHAPTER 92

At Last

What should I do next? The decision was complicated by the fact that I really didn't have any proof that Tyler was the prowler. That went out of the window when Mrs. Dawson couldn't identify Tyler from the yearbook photos. I thought about showing the same lineup to the woman whose panties he probably stole, but I immediately rejected that idea, knowing how DeSota and my sergeant would react.

So now what? Then I thought, *Suppose I got him to confess, to admit his guilt. Yes, it could work. But how? Where? At school? His house?*

Thinking about it, I realized that if someone else was present when I confronted Tyler, it might make him more defensive; my idea would work best if it was just the two of us. I figured that the most likely chance of meeting him would be after school but before he arrived home.

I decided that during tomorrow's shift, I would cruise Tyler's neighborhood from three o'clock on; I wanted to determine the street corners where the school bus stopped to drop off the local kids. Then, after the bus departed, if

I saw Tyler walking home alone, I'd stop him and have our discussion.

It sounded like a good plan, but it produced nothing. The next day, Tyler did not get off the bus near his house at the corner of Palm Meadow and Williamson. I looked for him again that night, but apparently I missed him or he hadn't ventured out.

The same thing happened the following day and evening. What was going on? I decided to give it one more try, and if he didn't show up on the bus that afternoon, I'd investigate where he was.

But then, success! I saw Tyler getting off the school bus, wearing long blue shorts, a white T-shirt, and his Jaguar's hat. But, damn it, he was walking along with some kid. A new complication.

I was still cruising slowly, about two blocks behind them, when I saw Tyler's companion peel off and enter a house. It was only three houses away from Tyler's, and I wasn't sure I could catch up with Tyler before he reached home.

Tyler was not yet to his house when I pulled up alongside of him, rolled down the passenger-side window, and yelled, "Hey, Tyler, come here a minute. I'd like to talk with you."

As he reluctantly walked toward the car, I turned on my body camera, got out of the car, and stood by the passenger door. When he walked up next to me, he seemed peeved. "Yeah, now what?" he whined.

I figured there might be some value in shock, so I decided to start out aggressively. Attempting to sound like a stern parent, I said, "Tyler, you lied to me."

He seemed startled. "What do you mean?"

"I asked you what you were doing out riding your bike at nine-thirty at night, and you told me you went to a basketball game at the junior high. I checked it out. Tyler, there was no basketball game that night at the school."

Tyler appeared dazed and a bit confused. He stumbled around, trying to come up with a response.

I pressed on, "Well, I *know* what you were doing. You were out prowling, probably looking for a house to rob."

"Look, man, what are you talking about? I wouldn't rob nobody."

"No? Then what were you doing?"

"I wasn't doing anything. Hey, leave me alone. I have to go."

"Tyler, listen to me. I talked with the lady who spotted you prowling in her yard. She called the police; we're on to you. What kind of things have you stolen?"

"This is crazy. I've never stolen anything. I was just peeping." Realizing that he had slipped up, Tyler wailed, "Oh, God, what am I going to do?" He started sobbing. "I didn't hurt anybody. Can I please go?"

"Tyler, we need to talk some more, but first I need to read you your rights."

I quickly took my rights card from my left-hand breast pocket and read it aloud. Tyler continued to sob.

"Did you understand what I read you?"

"Yeah."

"Tyler, you said that you didn't hurt anybody with your peeping, and you probably didn't, but I'd like to understand a little more about what you've been doing. What do you do when you peep?"

"Nothing. Just look at girls."

"Well, how many houses have you peeped at?"

"Oh, only a couple maybe. I didn't mean any harm."

"If I drive you around, could you find these houses? No one will see you point them out; I'd really like to know where they are."

"Okay, but can I go then?"

"We'll see."

"Okay, we're going to get in the car now and drive to the houses, but regulations require that I cuff you."

"Please don't. I'll cooperate."

"I know you will, Tyler, but the rules say that I'm required to do this. Now please turn around."

I cuffed him, patted him down, opened the back door, and guided him in.

As we drove along, I raised the dispatcher to advise her of each new address when we stopped and again when we were on the move. As Tyler pointed out the homes—there were three—I jotted down the house numbers and descriptions for my notes.

"Thanks for your help, Tyler."

There it was! I felt hyped. The prowler case was pretty much solved, even though I had heard about it only a few days ago.

I don't know what inspired me, but checking to be certain that my body camera was on, I asked Tyler another question. "Tyler, did you ever go into any of those houses?"

"Only one time."

"Which one of the three was it?"

"Oh, it wasn't one of them; it was a different place."

"A different house?"

"Yeah."

"Can you show me where it is?"

"Yeah."

"All right, tell me where to drive."

I gave dispatch my starting mileage and location. I had no idea where Tyler was going to take me.

CHAPTER 93

Surprise

Tyler directed me to proceed down Sandhill to Orchid and then turn right. When we came to the intersection with Seabrook, I almost died when he said, "Okay, turn right here on Seabrook."

As we proceeded down Seabrook, he said, "There it is. On the right—that gray one with the tile roof. It's got black shutters."

It was Nikki's house! I was so excited I almost couldn't speak, but I managed to radio in the mileage and address.

"That's the one you went in, number 481?"

"Yeah."

"How were you able to do that, get into the house?"

"It was sort of accidental. The back door was unlocked, and I just walked right in. But I didn't take anything."

"So," I asked, sounding puzzled, "what did you do in the house?"

"I walked around."

I didn't want to stop in front of Nikki's, so I continued driving slowly down Seabrook until I came to a vacant lot. I stopped the car and turned around to face Tyler.

He wouldn't look at me, and his shoulders were slumped. I remembered from my academy class on interrogative interviewing that this is a common behavior pattern when a guilty person is caught.

"Tyler, I'm curious. When you were walking around in there, did you move or touch anything?"

"I was going to have a soda, but I never got to drinking it."

"Did you take anything?"

"No," Tyler said with some irritation. "I told you before, I never took anything from anyplace."

"You're right; you did say that. Where else did you walk in the house?"

"I looked around in the big bedroom."

"Did you touch anything there?"

"Well, kinda."

"What did you touch?"

"Do I have to say?"

"No, Tyler, you don't have to say anything. I was just wondering."

"Well, you'll probably find out anyway. I opened a drawer and looked in at some underwear."

"Did you do anything else while you were in the bedroom?"

"No, I left and walked into the bathroom."

"What did you do there?"

"I traced a message with my finger on her bathroom mirror. I had seen a TV show where somebody did that, and I thought it was cool. I knew she wouldn't see it, but I would always know it was there."

I could not believe what I was hearing. I realized that I had just solved another case, one that had been haunting me since that first call to Nikki's, almost a year ago. I was so excited I almost couldn't think.

"I'm really interested. What did your hidden message say?"

"It said, 'I'll see you.'"

"And why those words?"

"'Cause that was my mission. I wanted to find out which window was for her bedroom, you know, so I could see her."

"Is she an attractive woman?"

"Sort of, but she's old, not a teenager."

"Tyler, I should tell you that in your peeping and breaking in, you broke several laws."

"Please don't tell my mom."

"I don't see how we can avoid it. You didn't intend to hurt anyone, you're a juvenile, and as far as I can tell, you haven't been in trouble before. So, I'm sure things will work out all right, but it's my job to bring you in. We'll have to go to the station and talk with the detective."

As we drove off to HQ, I still didn't believe what had just happened. After all that time, I finally nabbed the person who caused Nikki such agonizing worry. I could hardly wait to tell Sergeant Jordan.

CHAPTER 94

The Confrontation

I radioed dispatch and again gave starting mileage and advised that we were en route to the station. I also asked her to raise Detective DeSota and request him to meet me at the station. When I heard his sarcastic response, I knew the picnic was over.

I could envision DeSota ranting and tearing apart my findings, but I was consoled by the fact that I had Tyler's recorded confession, something I didn't think he'd be able to refute. Too bad I had to deal with him.

A few minutes later, when Tyler and I arrived at the station, I helped him out of the car, and as we walked inside, I saw Sergeant Jordan waiting in the hallway. He came toward us, looked at Tyler, and said, "Hello, young man," and then he added, "Jerry, get him checked in and put him in the interview room. We need to talk."

I did the processing with the booking sergeant and explained to Tyler that we'd get back to him shortly. I led him to the interview room, uncuffed him, and got him a soda. After locking the door, I found Sergeant Jordan at his desk.

"Jerry, I heard you on the radio with one in custody, and I heard you changing locations. So, I'm assuming the boy you brought in is our prowler."

"Sarge, not only is he our prowler, he's also our infamous panty raider!"

"No fucking way! Are you sure?"

"Yeah, I am. His confession is on my body camera, post Miranda too. I think I've got him."

"Well, congratulations, Jerry. Good work. I also heard you raise DeSota; I'm sure he's pissed. I bet he said something like 'Who the fuck does this rookie think he is, raising me and asking me to meet him!'"

My sergeant got this odd grin on his face and said, "Tell me all that happened, and then we'll go upstairs together. I don't want to miss this."

Making an effort to be succinct, I went through the whole stop. I played my recorded confession and showed him my notes about the locations, especially about Tyler's admission about the Coke can and the message on the mirror. As I unveiled the evidence, I was pleased to note that, every so often, the sarge said, "Good."

When we got off the elevator on the detective's floor, Sergeant Jordan hung back a step or two as we walked past a couple of other seated detectives until we reached Detective DeSota's desk. He was on the phone. We stood there till he ended the call.

DeSota looked up at me and, with an irritating voice, said, "Rookie, just how thickheaded are you? You don't ask me to meet you. I tell you! Is this about that Wilson woman? I swear, if you fuck up this case, I'll get you fired! What the fuck do you want?"

I knew he would be angry, so I wanted to get everything right the first time. I said, "I found the burglar. He's downstairs. Since you are the lead detective, I wanted to speak to you first."

His face almost crimson, DeSota stood up. I wasn't sure what to do. Automatically, I stretched out my left arm, fingers splayed, and said, "Detective, give me a second. Let me show you what I have."

Before he could respond, I started reading from my notes. I didn't want to look at him because I thought I would forget something important. I started to go through the Tyler stop and how he admitted to entering Nikki's house. But DeSota cut me off and said, "You are so fucking done. I'm going to enjoy watching you get fired. I told you not to fuck with my case!"

Suddenly, the room was silent. No one was talking; everyone was just staring at us. I could sense Sergeant Jordan walking closer to me.

DeSota looked past me and said to him, "You better get control of your people, Sarge!"

Clearly, my sergeant had had enough. From off my shoulder, I heard, "That's Sergeant to you, Detective. Now, let's do this my way, shall we? Get your ass into the conference room right now. I'm going to get Sergeant West, and we'll talk about this like gentlemen. Apparently, that's something that you have no knowledge of."

I could hear some suppressed laughs from the other detectives in the room. At that moment, the detective sergeant, Goldy West, came out of his office, apparently to check on the commotion he heard in his squad room. The two sergeants nodded at each other, and then my sergeant said, "Hi, Goldy. Will you join us for a few minutes in the conference room? I'm sure you'll find it very interesting."

Sergeant Jordan closed the conference room door and said to DeSota, "You don't deserve this, but I'm going to save you from further embarrassing yourself. So, sit down and shut up. It's the last favor I'm going to do for you. Oh, and don't ever tell me how to run my squad. You read me, tough guy?"

Turning toward me, Sarge said, "Jerry, please go through the whole story. Take your time and don't leave anything out. We want the lead detective here to have as much information as possible so he can close *your* case!"

More or less facing Sergeant West and sort of ignoring the detective, I presented my findings. Surprisingly, the room was quiet—the three men were attentive. And believe it or not, DeSota interrupted only once. I concluded the presentation by playing the body camera's sound of Tyler's confession.

To my surprise, the first one to speak was Sergeant West. "That's a damn fine job you did, young man. We need more rookies like you." I was flabbergasted at his compliment; it was the last thing I expected from him. Sarge added a word or two of praise, and I told DeSota that the break-in kid was downstairs in our interrogation room awaiting his interview. Then the two of us left.

As we were exiting the detective's desk area, we heard, from behind the half-open conference room door, Sergeant West beginning to unload on DeSota: "When are you going to stop being such a horse's ass?"

CHAPTER 95

What's Next

As we arrived at our floor and exited the elevator, I said, "Sarge, do you have a minute or two? I'd like to talk about Tyler."

"Sure, Jerry. Let's go to my office."

Once we were seated, I said, "I'm wondering what the next steps are with Tyler."

"Well, here's the likely scenario: First, DeSota will come down and interview him. He'll then contact Juvenile Services and review with them Tyler's background and the nature of the arrest. They'll probably say there is no need to incarcerate him and that his mother can take him home.

"DeSota will then track down his mother and explain that Tyler has been arrested and what he's been charged with. He'll also tell her that Tyler is here at the station and that she should come to pick him up. Before he's released, Tyler will be fingerprinted and photographed, and a DNA Bucal swab will be taken. A court date will also be set."

"And at court?"

"Since he has no prior record, in all likelihood they'll put him on probation, have a psychologist talk with Tyler, and set up a counseling program. Also, a social worker will visit the house and speak with Tyler's family and probably the neighbors.

"You know Jerry, your nabbing Tyler early on may have saved him from committing a more serious crime. Some time ago, a psychologist gave us a brief course about a study of serial rapists. She told us that most of them seem to live a normal life; they're married, have families, and maintain steady employment. But they often come from a dysfunctional family. Very few of them, for example, had close relationships with their mother or father, and a very high proportion were abused as children or adolescents. And get this, Jerry: many had an early history of fetish burglaries and peeping. In many ways, Tyler fits this mold. But the great thing is he'll now be getting counseling; it might prevent anything more serious from developing."

"Thanks, Sarge. I'm glad that the arrest served a good purpose. Before I head out for the rest of my shift, I'm going to stop by to see how Tyler's doing."

"Jerry, I'm proud of you. Solo on the job for less than a month, and you've solved two cases. It shows you have good instincts. I can't remember when a rookie has ever done that."

"Thank you, Sarge. I really credit the great training I've had."

"I know you did well at the academy and had excellent FTOs, but it was your persistence and instincts that brought about Tyler's confession. Now go out and finish your shift.

And, Jerry, it's all right to allow yourself a few pats on the back."

"Yes, sir."

"And, Jerry, as soon as you can, get cranking on your report. It's an important one. If you can draft a copy before tomorrow's shift, I'll review it with you, and we'll get if filed."

"Fine. I'll have it ready."

CHAPTER 96

Surprises

I started walking toward my car but then turned around and returned to the sergeant's office. His door was still open, and I said, "Sarge, I forgot to ask, but I wondered if DeSota will notify Nikki that we caught the guy who broke in."

"He should, but you can't count on it. If you want to tell her, go ahead."

"I think I might do that. Thanks, Sarge."

It was nearly six o'clock by the time I got back on patrol, but I was more energized than when I started out at two. I felt a heady sense of confidence, believing that I could handle any challenge thrown at me. The upbeat feeling was accompanied by the thought that my decision to become a cop was certainly the right one. I smiled as I anticipated the fun it would be telling Nikki about Tyler's arrest and describing to Bridge how the sergeant praised me for the capture.

While on my break, I called Bridge.

"Hi," she answered. "Great timing. I was just about to text you."

"Oh, what about?"

"I've got some exciting news. Will you be able to stop by my house when you finish your shift?"

"Sure, I could do that. But why don't you just tell me now?"

"I could," Bridge said, "but I want us to be together when I tell you."

"Sounds mysterious. The funny thing is the reason I called you was to say that I have something exciting to share with you."

"Tell me."

"No, I want us to be together when I tell you about it."

We both laughed. It was such a delight that we were almost always on the same wavelength.

"Okay," I said. "I'll see you a little after ten."

"Wonderful. Love you."

I couldn't imagine what Bridge's surprise was. I was so eager to meet her that I knew the next four hours were going to seem interminable.

CHAPTER 97

Great News

The instant Bridge opened her front door, we embraced. We were physically drawn to each another like opposite poles of a magnet. It was as though we needed to be one. There wasn't an instant of doubt that we were in love. Aside from that, I felt a little embarrassed that Bridge probably felt the stirring of my friend down below.

The Regan household, with Bridge's brother and two sisters, was usually a busy place, but tonight, all was quiet. "Where is everyone?" I asked.

"Oh yeah, it is quiet. Mom and Dad have gone to bed, and I think Sean is upstairs doing his homework. I don't know where my sisters are."

Bridge led me through the dining room to a screened-in patio. There was enough ambient light from the dining room to see the comfortable patio furniture, but otherwise it was dark. We stopped and hugged again. No words were spoken. We kissed hard and passionately. Our hands roamed.

Bridge reacted first. "Phew, Jerry, we better stop now—or we won't stop."

"Okay," I reluctantly agreed. It was not easy to do, but I respected Bridge's desire to hold off.

Bridge had set out, on a small cocktail table, a pitcher of cold tea and a few cans of iced Coke; we each plopped in a chair and took a few deep breaths.

"So," I said, "what's your surprise?"

Sounding a little breathless, she began, "I hardly know where to start; so many things have happened since we last talked. Well, as I was doing campus interviews, I had many opportunities to review the titles of classes that I would be required to take to get my teaching degree—"

"Yes," I interrupted, wanting her to get to the point.

"And, well, I wasn't at all excited about what I was seeing."

"So ..."

"So, I met with a career counselor at FB Community College, and after some testing and a few sessions, she helped me to see that my interests and skill sets were more appropriate for nursing than elementary school teaching. In a nutshell, I've decided to go into nursing!

"And, Jerry, there's more. I'm going to sign up for Mercy Hospital's nursing program. You take the required college courses at the FB Community College and, at the same time, take nursing classes at the hospital. So, what that means—and this is the most important part—I'm not going away to college. I'll be right here in Fortuna Beach!"

I could hardly believe what I was hearing. For months, as Bridge visited colleges, I had assumed that she was likely to select one where she'd get the college experience by living on campus in another state or pretty far away. Of course, that led to my fear of her meeting other guys and the potential of losing her.

"What a terrific decision! I can't tell you how happy that makes me. I think you'll make a great nurse, and best of all, we won't be separated. Bridge, I just don't have the words to explain how I feel; it's wonderful!"

"I thought my surprise would make you happy. That's why I wanted us to be together. I wanted the fun of seeing your reaction. Now, what is your news?"

I told her the story of Tyler and the accolades I received from Sarge. Then, to my surprise, I noticed that Bridge seemed serious, pensive. I wondered if she suddenly realized that in giving up a police career, she would never experience the thrill of the chase and the capture of the perp. But her pensiveness didn't last more than a few seconds. She brightened up, came out of her chair, sat on my lap, put her arms around my neck, and said, "Congratulations, Jerry. You're my hero!"

It was near midnight, and fatigue from a long and eventful day finally caught up with me; it was time to say good night. Neither one of us wanted to part, yet we did, but not without many "one more" kisses.

Driving home, I mused about the satisfying job I had, along with the wonderful bonus of knowing I'd be able to see Bridge almost daily. I was about as high as I imagined anyone could get without drugs or alcohol.

The next morning, I went in early and met the sarge. He reviewed my report on Tyler and made only a few revisions. The report-writing training I had gotten from Maria made all the difference.

At 1400 roll call, the sergeant complimented me on yesterday's "dogged pursuit and arrest of a subject." So, as I loaded my car, I was feeling upbeat—basking in my success—wondering what new experience this shift would bring.

As I was about to drive out of the station, the routine mumbling radio traffic was interrupted by an officer screaming, "One-three-two-two, one-three-two-two. Shots fired. Shots fired. One-three-two-two. Oh God, I've been hit!"

The beep tone went off, and the dispatcher said, "Officer shot. Officer down, 1700 Ocean Blvd. One-three-two-two is ten-fifty and down."

When I neared the gate and hit my lights and siren, I could see the station emptying as officers ran to their cars. Pushing the pedal down, my only thought was to get to 1322. Now!

About the Authors

John Drake is a psychologist and author. He has ten published books, including the best-selling and award-winning *Downshifting*, currently published in ten languages.

Earlier in life, John was the founder and CEO of one of the world's largest human resources firms—Drake Beam & Associates, Inc., now DBM—with offices worldwide. As a relatively young man, he sold this firm and established a mental health center as well as another firm of organizational psychologists. Finally, when he retired, he turned his talents to writing.

He holds a PhD in psychology and is a well-known consultant and lecturer in the corporate arena.

John and Dee Drake have four sons. They divide their time between Maine and Florida.

Kevin Kozak is a forty-two-year career law enforcement officer and US Air Force veteran. His assignments have included more than eighteen years of investigative experience with the largest police department in the state of Florida, a state attorney's office investigator, and a detective for a small Florida department. Kevin is SWAT certified. He now resides in Northeast Florida with his family, where he continues to serve his community and country and enjoys an occasional rum and lime juice on the beach.

Printed in the United States
By Bookmasters